"*Dragon Seed* unmasks and disarms the pride that so easily takes root in the heart. In the tradition of Lewis's *The Screwtape Letters*, Machowski retells the ancient saga of our defeated Enemy, through one family's spiritual battle. Between the page-turning plot and thought-provoking studies, teens and their parents will find much to discuss. It's divine truth through good story—one might even say, diabolically good."
  Champ Thornton, Author of *The Radical Book for Kids*

"In *Dragon Seed*, Marty Machowski pulls back the curtain to give us a creative and sobering look at the 'cosmic powers and spiritual forces of evil.' While the story is aimed at teenagers, adults would do well to reflect on its pages and the insidious nature of pride. I hope that readers young and old will pick up a copy of *Dragon Seed* to help them prayerfully consider the pride at work in their own hearts and give thanks to the One who ransomed those stony hearts."
  John Perritt, Resource Coordinator at Reformed Youth Ministries (rymonline.org); author of *Your Days Are Numbered* and *What Would Judas Do?*

"I gave my ten-year-old daughter a copy of *Dragon Seed*. Her mother caught her up an hour and a half past her bedtime still reading. When asked 'Why are you still up?' she replied, 'I couldn't put it down! I wanted to find out what happens next.' Need I say more? *Dragon Seed* captivated my daughter's imagination, as I'm sure it will with your own children.

In a day and age where Christian allegories are uncommon, Marty Machowski's *Dragon Seed* is a very welcome addition to our library. If you have a teen who shows you attitude, disrespect, and disregard, then *Dragon Seed* will be a help you and your kid. We all need help with fighting pride and cultivating humility. So read Marty's book along with your teen, so you can deal with the roots of pride taking over your own heart!"
  Deepak Reju, Pastor of Biblical C
  Ministry, Capitol Hill Baptis
  author of *On Guard: Preventi
  Abuse at Church* and *Preparin

"I recently read *Dragon Seed* together with three of my grandsons, Daniel (12), Silas (13), and Matthew (14). Through this fascinating story, the boys gained a renewed understanding of the gospel and the horror of pride. I strongly recommend *Dragon Seed* for teens and young adults."

William Farley, Author of *Gospel Powered Parenting*

"My two boys and I loved *Dragon Seed*. Our imaginations and hearts have been stirred by its distinct message so creatively wrapped in a great story. It has led to significant conversations about the awfulness of rebellion against God and the dangers of letting the 'seed' take root in our hearts. Parents, don't hesitate! Read this together with your adolescent . . . indeed, Nick's struggles are familiar to all of us."

Barry Joslin, Professor of Christian Theology, Boyce College, The Southern Baptist Theological Seminary, Louisville, KY

"My middle school daughter was hooked. For any pre-teen or teenager who loves an adventure story, *Dragon Seed* is a page turner. And the best part is this story is true! In this captivating story, Marty Machowski makes clear that pride is no respecter of persons—its seeds infect both religious and irreligious. There is only one antidote, the love and sacrifice of our carpenter Savior. I highly recommend this book for your kids."

Jared Kennedy, Pastor of Families at Sojourn Community Church—Midtown in Louisville, KY; author of *The Beginner's Gospel Story Bible*

Dragon Seed

Marty Machowski

newgrowthpress.com

New Growth Press, Greensboro, NC 27401
Copyright © 2017 by Marty Machowski

All rights reserved. No part of this publication may be reproduced, stored in a retrieval system, or transmitted in any form by any means, electronic, mechanical, photocopy, recording, or otherwise, without the prior permission of the publisher, except as provided by USA copyright law.

Unless otherwise indicated, Scripture quotations are taken from The Holy Bible, English Standard Version.® Copyright © 2000; 2001 by Crossway Bibles, a division of Good News Publishers. Used by permission. All rights reserved.
    Scripture quotations marked NIV are taken from THE HOLY BIBLE, NEW INTERNATIONAL VERSION®, NIV® Copyright © 1973, 1978, 1984, 2011 by Biblica, Inc.® Used by permission. All rights reserved worldwide.

Cover Design: Faceout Books, faceoutstudio.com

ISBN 978-1-945270-00-0 (Print)
ISBN 978-1-945270-01-7 (eBook)

Library of Congress Cataloging-in-Publication Data on file

Printed in India

31 30 29 28 27 26 25 24   3 4 5 6 7

*I would like to dedicate this book to my children
and offer it as a gift to the generations who follow in their footsteps.
May they pass it down to their children,
and their children's children after them.*

To: Nathan and Lauren, Emma and Destin, Martha, Noah, Anna, and Amelia

*"Things that we have heard and known,
that our fathers have told us.
We will not hide them from their children,
but tell to the coming generation
the glorious deeds of the LORD, and his might,
and the wonders that he has done." (Psalms 78:3–4)*

*Yours truly,
Tymar*

Table of Contents

Acknowledgments	ix
Introduction	xi
1. The Voice of the Shadow	1
2. The Birth of the Dragon	8
3. The Mutiny of the Dragon	14
4. The Fall of the Dragon	20
5. Planning Revenge	26
6. The Dragon's Temptations	33
7. The Curse	39
8. The Spread of the Seed	45
9. The Prophecy	51
10. The Arrival of the Maharajahs	57
11. To the City of the Giant Slayer	64
12. The Prince Is Discovered	70
13. Temptation in the Wilderness	77
14. The Man of the Tombs	82
15. Into the Swine	92
16. The Rescue	99
17. Trouble in the Temple City	108
18. Stuck Behind Bars	114
19. The Dragon's Revenge	119
20. Victory	125
21. A Return to the Well	132
22. The Revelation	137
23. The End of the Story	142

The Antidote

Day One: The First Law of Pride	146
Day Two: The Second Law of Pride	149
Day Three: The Power of Desire	152
Day Four: Who Will Represent You?	155
Day Five: The Prophecy Is True	158
Day Six: Humility: The Antidote to Pride	161
Day Seven: God Knows Your Struggle	164
Day Eight: No One Is Invincible	167
Day Nine: True Greatness	169
Day Ten: His Story Is History	172
Day Eleven: What No Other Man Has Done	175
Day Twelve: Humility Kills the Dragon	177

Acknowledgments

While I get my name on the cover, it is important to acknowledge the many folks who read through early manuscripts and offered their kind, helpful critique. In that regard I would like to thank Chris Patton, Eric Holter, Ken Mellinger, Aaron Mayfield, Greg Dirnberger, Josh Blount, Champ Thornton, Jason Stowel, Linda Redrup, Bryan DeWire, Sheila Nottage, Brian Kaufman, and Joel Shorey. I would also like to thank the pastoral team at Covenant Fellowship, whose consistent encouragement is a means of grace to keep me writing. Thank you Anna and Amelia, my two youngest daughters, for insisting that I keep working and publish "their favorite book that I have ever written." And of course my wife, who allows me to wake her up early in the morning so that I can read the latest ending to a chapter. Thank you Joemel Requezza for your amazing cover illustration. Finally, I would like to thank the New Growth Press team for your support and partnership in publishing.

Introduction

An allegory is a story that contains a hidden meaning. The following story is my idea of how the angels' mutiny in heaven against God and the spread of evil through the earth below might have happened. In presenting this fictional tale, I do not want to contradict anything the Bible teaches, but rather use the creative genre of allegory to capture your imagination. The Bible itself uses an apocalyptic allegory in presenting Satan as a dragon, bent on devouring the Christ child (Revelation 12:4). It is this imagery that I borrow from and expand on in *Dragon Seed*. It is critical that we learn to recognize the dragon's scheming ways and his temptations, for they are the greatest danger we will ever face.

Artists paint with oil on canvas. Writers paint with words on a page—stirring the imagination. While we remain anchored to Scripture as our final authority, I invite you to join me on an allegorical journey. Within these pages, we will imagine what it might have been like to see the cherubim of heaven go to war against the throne and watch the dragon rise to power to seek his full revenge against the King.

Chapter 1

The Voice of the Shadow

"You can't tell me what to do!"

Nick Freeman thundered past a pile of books at the edge of the living room, his stride sending the stack flying as he stormed down the hall. "I already said I was just down the street at Tony's. I'm not a baby, Mom!"

A faint shadow swirled above him, but only his grandmother, who sat just out of the way in the corner rocker, noticed.

Mary shouted back at her son, "You know better than to speak to me that way, Nick! This conversation is far from over. If you think it's okay to just leave the house at all hours of the night, you've got another think coming!"

"I can leave if I want. Don't try to stop me!"

As the door to his room slammed shut and cut off his words, she sank to the couch with hands shaking. Breathing rapidly, she closed her eyes.

"Lord! I don't know how many more of these fights I can take! Why do I have to face these teenage years alone?"

"Oh, sweetie," a soft voice broke through Mary's stormy thoughts. "I'm so sorry this hurts so bad. But honey, you are the opposite of alone in this." Anna Cummings had been quietly praying as her daughter woke up that Saturday morning in a frenzy after not finding Nick in his bed. It had taken her an hour of calling friends and neighbors to figure out where he was. And the argument that had followed his indifferent reentry into the house was not for the faint of heart. "We've got to figure out some actions-steps here, Mary."

"Why did God have to take Matt from us so early, Mom? Nick adored him. Every word he said was gold. I thought with time Nick would start to heal and start to find things to smile about again. But ever since he turned fifteen, his anger has just exploded at everything around him—especially me."

"A gentle answer turns away wrath," The elderly woman replied. "It's obvious Nick is at a crossroads here, Mary. He's going to have make a choice about his anger. He needs to know his mom is not his enemy."

Mary turned to answer her mom, whose crackled but kind voice calmed her. She sat covered with a crocheted comforter. "I'm afraid. He's been staying out later and later. I don't like the influence his friends are having on him. And that kid knows how to push my buttons," she said. "What am I supposed to do?"

"You know what to do."

"I don't know what to do, Mom." She ran her hands through her hair, then stepped into the foyer which connected the two rooms and hall. "Was I this stubborn as a child? Was it this hard?"

Anna smiled. "Harder. It always feels harder when it is your own child. But remember, it is hard for Nick too."

She let those words sink in for a moment, then added, "I think it's time for you to pass on the story." With those words a second shadow fled down the hall.

Mary paused, "I've thought about it. But what if it doesn't work or if he thinks I'm trying to tell him what to do? What if he makes fun of it? What if he doesn't read it?"

"He'll read it. You remember how the story takes hold of you. Plus, it becomes a scary story when you realize that it is not just a tale; that it is real. Teenagers love a scary story. It is not every family that has a legend to pass on to its children."

"Do you think it's true?" Mary had always wanted to ask her mom that question.

"The story? I know it's true."

"Not the story. The part about how we got the story," Mary said.

"Doesn't much matter if he was our great far-off grandfather or not. He was someone's great far-off grandfather, living among the tombs, possessed by evil, hearing voices all the day long until he was set free."

"But do you think it's true? Was the story passed down from him, or was it made up by your father or grandfather?"

"My father passed it to me, saying his father passed it to him. That is all I know," Anna said, and then continued, "I believe it's true. I've seen a shadow lurking about that boy. Give him the book, Mary. The time is right. You must give it in the right season, you know. Pass it on too early and children forget it. Pass it on too late—well, then it is just too late. But I think the time is right now. The shadow is already filling his heart. That is why it is so easy for him to disrespect you. And yet he is not so far given over that he won't read the story."

"I don't know—are you sure?"

"Go on, you know where we keep it," she said and pointed to the center of the brick fireplace.

Mary walked across the room to the left side of the fireplace. She slid out the last brick on the left, which sat directly under the massive oak mantel. She slipped her hand into a cavity, and pulled down a thin, dark brown book.

"Okay, Mom," she said as she rubbed her index finger across the leather-bound cover. She remembered the day when, as a thirteen-year-old, the story had been passed on to her. Back then, she had taken the book from her father's hand, intending not to read it. She had been angry too, but curiosity compelled her to turn the first pages. Then the story drew her in.

She couldn't bear the thought of losing Nick. For a moment she stood paralyzed, too afraid to walk down the hall to Nick's room but even more fearful to return the book to its hideaway.

*****

Nick pounded his fist against his bedroom door. The shadow swirled about him, but he didn't sense its presence.

"I'm sick of this. I can't do anything around here."

"You're older now. You're not in kindergarten anymore. She doesn't let you do anything. You could just sneak out again later. What could she say?" The tempting words spewed from the shadow, filling Nick's thoughts, playing on his desires.

Nick slipped his backpack off his shoulder, dropped to his knees, and reached into the half-zipped main compartment. Two heavy schoolbooks crashed against the wall as he emptied the pack. Into the void he stuffed a sweatshirt that was clumped up next to his dresser. Looking over to the door, he eyed the center of the knob. He half crawled a step, stretched his arm far out, and turned the lock with a flip of his finger.

"If Tony goes, I go," Nick said to himself. Digging further in the bag, he pulled out a phone with a web of cracks across the screen and slipped it into his pocket. *What Mom doesn't know won't hurt her.*

"You're a smart man, Nick," the shadow whispered.

Nick stood to his feet and paced up and down the football rug next to his bed. Suddenly the toe of his shoe tripped on a hidden sock stuffed underneath and sent him stumbling forward across his beanbag chair into his desk. Anger bubbled up to the surface as he blurted a few choice words.

"Stupid rug! Stupid room!" he bellowed. He reached to the open desk drawer next to his window and pulled out a two-toned golf ball that had started rolling around. It was all he could do to not throw it straight through the window in disgust.

*****

Mary, encouraged by her mother's words, walked the long central hall to her son's bedroom door. Her footsteps sounded on the wooden floor, announcing her approach.

"Hey Nick, it's Mom," she said loud enough to carry through the hollow bedroom door.

"What do you want?" he growled as he pulled the phone out of his pocket. He slid it and the golf ball under his pillow.

"We need to talk. For a few more minutes."

Nick looked around the room, kicked his pack aside, then unlocked and opened the door. He briefly caught her expression, then looked away from his mom and sighed.

"There's that look of disrespect. You've seen it a thousand times." The shadow spoke the temptation to Mary as she stood before the open door.

"I wish you wouldn't lock the door on me," she said.

"It's your door." The shadow whispered to Nick.

It's my door. I'll lock it if I want, Nick owned the thought, and rolled his eyes in disgust. "Sometimes I like the door locked," he said.

Mary took a deep breath, and paused before she spoke. "Look, I don't want to start arguing again. You've got to figure out what you're going to do about this disrespect. This is a real problem that's not going to just go away. But right now, I'm not here to talk about that. Can I just sit down and show you something?" Her calmer, steady tone, in spite of Nick's harsh words, caught him off guard. His shoulders relaxed. The shadow shrunk back.

"All I want to talk about right now is you not watching my every move like you're the police or something. It's not like I'm two and need you to arrange all of my little playdates."

"Nick, I don't think your attitude is a wise choice."

"Whatever."

Mary took another steadying breath and lowered herself to the edge of Nick's bed, holding out the book. "I've been waiting to give this to you," she said simply.

"What is it?"

"A book. Mom-Mom calls it our family legend. This story has been passed down through our family. I think it's time you take a look at it. You want to be treated like you're older? Well, here's the first step. Read it. It's been in our family for generations."

"What's it about?"

"Dragons and things," she said as she moved it closer still.

"Dragons? Our family has a dragon story?" The thought seemed a little ludicrous, yet the idea of a family legend intrigued him.

"Your dad liked it too. Take a look for yourself." Mary handed the book to her son.

Nick felt the well-worn cover. It was soft. It smelled like an old box that had been in the attic. The book drew his curiosity, and he had always loved to read.

"Will you read it?" Mary looked into her son's eyes, hoping he would say yes.

A part of Nick wanted to say no, but would this get his mom off his back for awhile? It might be worth skimming a few pages just to get a break from the nagging. Plus, something about her tone had changed from their fight in the living room. Her calm, steady gaze was like a foot in the door to his heart, preventing him from shutting it tight against her.

Nick paused, glanced into his mother's eyes, and answered, "I'll read it." He jerked the book from his mother's hand, then burrowed into the corner of his bed, signaling her to leave. As she stood and started back down the hall, he shook a nagging thought from the corner of his heart. *You didn't need to yank it from her.*

Back outside the door, a tear coursed down the side of Mary's face. She paused and called back, "Thanks Nick." Then she turned and made her way back to the front of the house.

Nick glanced down and read the cover. *Dragon Seed*? He flipped the book to the first page of the story. The opening chapter started with "Introductions." *So far, so boring*, he thought. But he kept reading anyway.

Chapter 2

The Birth of the Dragon

With his thumb marking the page, Nick settled in against his headboard and looked down at the handwritten text. The pages were so yellow that he would have to be careful how he turned them. Then the first words caught his eye:

You, my reader, are in danger. Pay attention carefully to what I'm about to tell you. You may already be infected. Have the seeds of darkness already begun to sprout in you?

Nick sat up with a slight shiver.

I, Tymar, write these words in my own hand. Within these pages, I'm passing to you my great far-off grandfather's story. People called him the man of the tombs. The account of his life has been passed from generation to generation within our family by spoken word. But it is not just his story. It is my story, and it is yours. That is why it cannot be forgotten and why I have taken it upon myself to write down all that my father shared with me. I am confident the story has not yet lost its power, for it has penetrated my heart and transformed my life. It is my prayer it will do the same for you.

When the tale is done, pay attention to the end. You will want to know what to do, how to protect yourself. I've assembled a collection of studies I call "The Antidote." When you've finished the story, you'll better understand the danger you face. The Antidote will give you vital information: how to arm yourself for the battle at hand, and what to do if you find the dragon's seed in your own heart. These studies are as important as the story itself. I implore you to resist the temptation to skip over them.

Now, let me start by telling you about the nature of seeds.

Perhaps you know how seeds grow. They are tiny specks, but once planted in the ground, when everything is just right, they sprout and grow into flowers, vegetables, and trees. The seeds look very different from what they become. An acorn is like a shiny ball wearing a brown hard hat, which you can hide in the palm of your hand, but it grows to become a mighty tree giving shade to all beneath its branches. A delicate dandelion seed can fly for miles, like a hot air balloon on the wind. But once it lands it sends a root deep into the ground and spreads wide leaves to kill the nearby grass. Some seeds, you see, look pretty but cause great damage when they grow.

But there is one seed, the seed of pride, which is the most terrible of all. It can remain upon the earth for a thousand years and never sprout a root, for it needs the tender soil of a human heart to grow. But should pride land upon a heart, it sends a deep and terrible root and grows into a horrid monster. That is why it bears the name dragon seed.

Today these seeds float everywhere around us, and once a dragon seed lands on a heart, it sprouts in minutes. Think of a dragon seed like pokeweed seed. When a pokeweed seed sprouts, it is a tiny plant with a little root you can pull with little effort. If it remains hidden under a bush or around a corner and is allowed to grow, however, it sends a strong carrot-like root deep into the soil. Even if you grasp it low it snaps off at the ground and the root keeps growing.

So it is with dragon seed sprouting in the heart. As a small prideful thought, it can be plucked out, but if allowed to grow, it twists and bends the mind toward evil. Jealousy sprouts; a root of blinding arrogance plunges deep. Then a lying tongue forms, and from that the entire course of life for that person changes. Like a small rudder on a ship, the lying tongue turns a person's life away from God, and the ugly scales of bitterness, envy, hatred, lust, and anger begin to form.

It wouldn't be too alarming if dragon seed was uncommon and my experience with it rare. Unfortunately, though, dragon seed is everywhere and all around us. Anywhere you see a shadow swirl, you can be sure that dragon seeds are on the wind. Just like dandelion seeds they float, eager to land and sprout on the smallest patch of earth. We are helpless to avoid them, and dragon seeds seem to outsmart the cleverest minds. Our only hope is that the Prince, true to the promise, will kill the dragon and destroy his seeds once and for all.

Oh, have I not told you? There is a real dragon; he was the first to allow pride to sprout up in his heart. The dragon seeds that plague us today find their origin in him. A long time ago, before the first dragon seed was formed, every creature worshiped the King of the Mountain. Their songs echoed for a thousand miles. The guardians of the mountain throne sang the most beautiful songs and served the King's every wish.

The King's guardians formed the strongest and most magnificent army ever created. Their snowy white wings spanned thirty feet wide tip to tip. Silken robes flowed from their shoulders under a highly polished breastplate of bronze. The soft ripples of fabric were cinched at the waist by a wide golden band. The arms and legs of the smallest of the guards appeared as though they were made of iron or chiseled of granite, popping with muscles.

But on one fateful day the lead guardian made a grave mistake. He turned his gaze away from the throne to admire himself. As he delighted in his own beauty, his heart grew cold toward the king. The very first dragon seed of pride formed within his heart, then it sprouted and sent black roots to invade the core. That was the day the first dragon was born.

*****

Nick finished reading the introduction and turned the page, unable to help himself. Curiosity was getting the better of him.

Outside the back door Mia sent off a quick text then dropped her phone out of sight back into her purse and pressed the doorbell. Back in the main part of the house, the doorbell rang a two-toned note, breaking the tentative quiet that had settled on the house. Martha, Nick's older sister, flung open her bedroom door, bounded down the hall, and poked her head into the kitchen.

"That must be Mia. I'm heading out, Mom."

Mary turned away from the sink toward her daughter. "Heading out? Mia? I thought you were just out studying with her two days ago. I hardly ever see you anymore."

"Mom. I was home all day yesterday after school. It's not like I've been traipsing all over the place or anything," Martha couldn't help but get that small dig in. She sighed. "You know I told you Mia needed help in American Government. We couldn't get through everything on Thursday."

"I didn't know you were going over today. Do you have a test?"

"No, I don't have a test. You know me. I like to study as we go along. That way I don't have to worry when the test comes. Gotta keep those grades up. That's what . . . "

"I know. That's what your father used to say. You're just going over to study, right?"

"Of course, Mom. No need to worry. I am not sneaking out anywhere. We're going to go over our American Government. Mia's not doing well. She tells me the class is too boring. Helping her helps me. Can I go? Mia's at the door." Martha didn't feel like she needed to ask again, but she could see her mom was still worked up over the fight with Nick.

Mary offered her a little smile. "Okay. Don't be too late."

Martha gave her mom a quick hug. Then the doorbell sounded again.

"Gotta go. Bye, Mom-Mom," Martha called over her shoulder. Her grandmother waved and said goodbye.

"I'll try to be home for dinner, but you know how that is with Mrs. Rossi."

"Have a good time," Mary replied. Martha lifted a backpack up from the floor, hoisted it over her shoulders, and then took off running for the front door.

"Why couldn't Nick be more like Martha? Why does he have to give me so much grief?" Mary said quietly as she watched Martha pull the door closed and run to the waiting car with her friend.

Anna pushed herself up from the cushioned rocker and corrected her daughter, "Don't be so quick to criticize Nick."

"What am I supposed to do? He snuck out of the house without saying a word. He wasn't in his bed this morning. He could have been out all night for all I know. Mom, Martha gets straight A's. She left to go study with Mia. . . ."

"I know, dear." The older woman understood her daughter's frustration and waited patiently for an opportunity to encourage her.

"They don't even have a test, for crying out loud. Nick doesn't study when he has a test!"

"Mary, comparing Martha and Nick isn't helpful. They're two completely different kids, with two different lives. Nick is not so far gone as you think, and Martha has her own challenges. Ever since her father died, she's found her identity in getting perfect grades. That's not good either. Academics won't save her."

"Look. I'm trying to deal with Nick. Martha is going to be alright. She's got solid friends and is doing so well in school and gymnastics. If she doesn't get an academic scholarship, she may just get one for gymnastics. I'm telling you, Nick is the one we've got to worry about."

"That's just it, Mary. You need to trust God and give him your worries. You know he cares for you—and for your children. Come over here."

Mary walked closer to her mom. Anna took her hand and gave it a gentle squeeze.

"A moment ago you walked into this room so grateful Nick accepted the book to read. Don't let worry steal your joy. Let the book do its work. God is after that boy," she said encouragingly. "You'll see."

Chapter 3

The Mutiny of the Dragon

Still in his room, oblivious to his mom's worries, and almost despite himself, Nick stretched out on his bed and kept reading.

*****

Fresh blooming roses scented the air. The song of a mighty chorus rang out in all directions.

The light beaming from the throne pierced through everything. There were no shadows atop the mount. The light passed right through the nearby marble pillars and other gilded furnishings, painting a kaleidoscope of colors everywhere. Morningstar, the lead guardian of the King, never tired of the beautiful display.

Each of the guardians encircling the throne bore four wings. The thunder from their vibrating wings echoed against the rock of the mountain below. With four faces, the guardians watched in all directions. With their cherubim faces, they looked toward the throne and sang. Their human face looked to the right, the image of a lion to the left, and that of an eagle to the rear.

The throne sat in the exact center on a floor of a polished white marble. The King sat on the throne, the Prince stood to his side, and the Spirit of the King hovered as a Dove over the King and his Son. All three smiled their approval as the ring of guardians revolved around the throne. One by one the cherubs passed in review before the King and as they did the eyes of each met those of the king. In that moment the presenting cherub experienced an indescribable joy.

The King surely loved his Son, the Prince, who joined the song of the guardians, singing praises to the King. The Prince sang the sweetest melody while the Spirit above added harmony to the song. The guardians surrounding the throne took turns singing the melody with the Prince or harmony with the Spirit.

Morningstar sang the melody as he passed directly in front of the King. He fixed his gaze upon the King and felt the familiar joy-filled love pouring from the throne. Then as the ring of guardians turned, the King locked his gaze upon the next of his cherubim guards, the one directly to the right of Morningstar. Though his heart should have remained overflowing with delight, something had changed. On the outside he sang the King's praises with the rest of the guardians, but inside his heart was growing cold and indifferent. He simply repeated the phrases of the song out of habit. A seed took root in his heart, and for the first time one of the King's creatures wanted more than to worship the King. Morningstar looked at himself, felt pride in his own strength and beauty. He wanted the cherubim to notice him.

As the mighty army of cherubs worshiped, Morningstar pulled his gaze away from the throne and glanced to check the left and right of the formation. Loyalous, the second in command, kept guard at the opposite side of the arc of guardians. Loyalous fixed his cherub eyes upon the throne and never turned to the left or right—perhaps that is why he did not notice Morningstar's odd behavior.

Morningstar hatched a terrible plan. It would start with getting the other cherubim to notice and follow him. He planned each word of his address. Deep in his heart the seed that sprouted began to burrow its evil shoots down to his core. Even now he could have pulled the sprout, but instead he let the thick root go deeper still.

He paused his singing and called to the mighty army with a roaring voice.

"Look to me, my mighty cherubim!" Morningstar commanded.

Not a single guardian moved. Their focus remained fixed upon the throne and their singing continued uninterrupted.

Morningstar repeated his command, "Look to me, my mighty cherubim!"

While those further away continued their psalm of praise, a few of those immediately to the right glanced at Morningstar with their left-facing lion eyes, and those to the left stole a peek through their human faces. Nothing like this had ever occurred before. The cherubim trusted their commander, but didn't understand why he wanted to draw their attention away from the throne.

Morningstar continued his address, "Hear me, my mighty cherubim, guardians of the King's throne. Day after day we stand guard for the King. We are a mighty army ever staring at the throne ahead and guarding against attack by some unseen enemy to the rear."

The cherubim hovered, wingtip to wingtip in formation, trying to make sense of Morningstar's unusual address. And then it happened: Morningstar broke rank, shot high above, and turned his back to the throne saying, "Look at me." As he issued the command, he spread all four of his wings, exposing his iron-strong arms. With each of his two hands, he made a fist and lifted them high into the air.

"We are the mighty cherubim of the mountain!" Evil, dark seeds spewed from his mouth as he shouted, peppering the guardians directly below. The seeds fell, working their way down into the hearts of the cherubim who were looking toward him. Some sprouted instantly.

Several cherubs turned their gaze from the throne toward their commander. Morningstar's beauty amazed them. He stood taller than the other guardians; his breastplate glistened as bright polished bronze. The feathers of his wings reflected a rainbow of colors. The heavy brow of his cherubim face conveyed a confident strength while his long silvery beard made him seem wise.

His voice thundered as he spoke. "Now turn and greet those around you and see for yourself that each of you, down to the last, are adorned with beauty and strength the same as I," Morningstar said, spewing more and more evil seeds upon the unsuspecting guardians.

Those who obeyed his command realized that they too were beautiful and strong. As they admired themselves, the seeds of pride sprouted and grew. While none matched the strength of Morningstar, the least of their number bore the strength of ten men. One by one others affected by the seeds joined in, and chatter broke out as the guardians of the mountain delighted in their created beauty.

Lowly and Lumenon, the nearest two commanders under Morningstar's charge, broke rank and flew to Morningstar's side, bowing allegiance to their leader, giving him their loyalty.

Perfect, Morningstar thought to himself. *Just as I suspected—pride is infectious!*

Those cherubim further out to the left and right did not move, for the reach of Morningstar's voice against the praises of the King was limited. This limitation should have been an indication to Morningstar of his weakness, for whenever the King spoke, everyone could hear his voice, even above the praise.

"Join with me," Morningstar said to those within reach of his voice. "The King enthroned above has placed us as his guardians, to worship before his throne. We stand guard against a faceless enemy—one that does not exist. I tell you, the King knows that as long as we believe there is a threat beyond our borders, he holds control over us. You've seen nothing with your eagle eyes all the day, nor have you ever."

The guardians listening nodded in agreement. A few more broke rank—some from Lowly's command, some from Lumenon's—and joined the growing rebellion.

"You've known since the King of the Mountain created us that no force formed against the heavens could prevail. For we are the mighty cherubim." Morningstar lifted his head and displayed a confident smirk as he scanned the growing mob.

The guards in front all nodded again. Still more guardians flew to his side.

Morningstar lifted his arms, spread his wings, and shouted, "No one, not even the King, can stand against us." As Morningstar spoke, he looked down upon his strong forearms. Fresh dragon seed sprouted, sending roots of bitterness, hatred, and revenge down deep. His arrogant rebellion against the King spread dragon seed to a third of the mountain guard. They too began to admire themselves and their strength as they unsheathed their swords and swiped them through the air to the left and right. Murmuring and complaining spread among the company, and several of the guardians shouted accusations against the King for placing them in such slavery. The infected cherubim mob began to talk of revenge.

Morningstar smiled but didn't notice that the light beaming from the throne no longer passed through him. Throughout the mountaintop, the light passed without effort through all that was good. Morningstar also didn't know that shadows could not stand in the realm of the King. A hint of shadow now formed behind him.

"Rally to me, my comrades. I am the morning star!" With that bold claim, Morningstar charged the throne, his sword lifted high above his head. A full third of the cherub guards followed with swords drawn, ready to attack. The remaining loyal guardians re-formed a ring around the throne. They discerned the mutiny and waited for the King's command to engage the advancing rebel forces.

*****

Bzzzzzz. Bzzzzzzz. Bzzzzzzz.

Nick was jolted out of the story by the vibrating sound. He dropped the book and jumped up from the floor searching for his phone.

Bzzzzzz. Bzzzzzzzz. Bzzzzzz.

"The pillow!" Nick turned toward the bed, dug under the spot where he'd been sitting, and grabbed the phone before the noise had a chance to alert anyone else in the house. Shadows hovering above circled wildly, the interruption from the forbidden phone signaling a prime opportunity. In their excitement they abandoned their disguise, and the shadows took shape. They were dragons.

Chapter 4

The Fall of the Dragon

"Tony," Nick whispered harshly into the phone, "I told you to just text, not call. If I got caught with this phone, it would be over." Bitterlous and Arrogance, Nick's assigned dragons, circled above like two vultures over a kill.

"I know, but I needed an answer. And I never know when you're going to check your texts. So, are you coming to the party tonight? Everybody's gonna be there. Derrick's parents aren't coming home till tomorrow night."

"Listen, I don't know how I'm gonna sneak past Mom again," Nick stifled a loud sigh. You shoulda heard her wailing on me just for being at your house this morning! It's like she thinks she owns me."

The dragons swooped down to listen in on the conversation, flying tight circles around his head, close enough to deliver their temptations.

Bitterlous spoke first. *"You're not in kindergarten anymore. You can make your own decisions. Your mom will just have to get over it."*

"Yeah, man, you got quite an old lady there, watchin' you like a hawk or somethin'," Tony's voice crackled over the phone. "Think it over. This chance might not come up again for months."

Bitterlous smiled, sensing a victory. The two dragons eyed one another, swirling like a dark tornado over the boy.

"Come on," Tony pleaded with Nick. "Live a little."

Arrogance swooped in. *"You're already stuck at home. What more could she do to you anyway?"*

"I mean, I don't know how much worse things could get anyway," Nick conceded. "I'm not in kindergarten anymore. I can make my own decisions. She's already taken my video games away till my grades come up. Oh, yeah. And she gave me some dumb book to read." He glanced down at the book off to the side of his bed.

"Look, I'll see what I can do. I'll text you by five if I think of a way outta this place."

Nick glanced at his phone and noticed a missed text.

"Of course," he mumbled to himself. "I can't believe she was here and I missed her." He shot her back a response.

Then he thought about the party and what he should say, then sent a second text.

I'm trying to figure out a way to get around my mom.

Nick shoved the phone back under the pillow and absently reached for the golf ball he'd dropped next to the bed. The more he tossed it up into the air, the more his mind swirled with resentment and frustration.

Well, let's at least play her game for this afternoon. If I act like I'm interested in her little book, maybe she'll leave me alone and I can figure out what to do. He settled back against the headboard and found the page where he left off. He'd give it a chapter or two more. The family legend thing did prick a bit of his curiosity, but he thought it could be just a trick to get him to read some moralistic story. He held the ball in his right hand as he read, rolling it around in his fingers.

*****

As Morningstar flew higher, he looked down at the ring of loyal forces, holding their position. *I thought for sure I'd face a greater opposition*, he mused.

Fooled by the lack of counterattack, Morningstar imagined a quick and decisive victory. But Morningstar celebrated prematurely, for as he sped toward the throne, he cast a shadow behind.

The instant the shadow appeared, as quick as a flash of lightning, light from the King's throne threw Morningstar and all his rebel forces backward. Then, with one nod from the King, the loyal cherub army flew forward toward the rebels. Loyalous, their new commanding cherub, directed his forces to draw their fiery swords and attack the mutinous forces. The defending cherubs shouted in unison, "Glory and power belong to the King." With those words their swords burst forth with radiant light, but the swords of the rebels did not shine. As the two forces met, the crash of their swords thundered in the heavens.

The holy light of heaven burst forth again from the King, seated on the throne. The evil forces screamed as the light burned their flesh with each attempt to advance against it. Again and again they tumbled backward. Morningstar fought against the light and managed to thrust his sword at Loyalous who met him head-on in battle.

Loyalous crashed his blade against the advancing sword of Morningstar, ripping it from his hand with one blow. The weapon tumbled down out of reach and fell to the lowlands below. With a return swipe, Loyalous slashed the breastplate of the once mighty companion, throwing Morningstar backward through the air.

The pure light of the throne burned the feathers from their wings and cast the rebel forces ever downward. The humiliation of their defeat turned their dragon hearts to stone, locking their black roots of pride inside them forever. Fear and bitter anger filled their minds.

The loyal forces remained on top of the mountain and did not pursue them. They returned to the throne and re-formed a guardian ring around the King. Not a single loyal cherub received so much as a scratch in the battle. Nor were they the least bit exhausted from the effort, for it was the light beaming from the throne that had repelled the enemy forces.

In his pride, Morningstar had convinced his fellow mutineers there were no enemy forces—that they guarded against a fictitious enemy. In the end he became the very enemy he was commissioned to oppose. He also misjudged the true purpose of the guardians. The King needed no protection. The cherubim stationed by the King were created to adorn the King's mountain and demonstrate a picture of his greatness and strength.

The rebels, blackened and humiliated, fell and fell and fell until a great abyss of fire and torture opened like a giant mouth and swallowed them whole. The rebel cherubim screamed in painful torment as they crashed down upon blistering coals, which charred their flesh. The fire scarred, burned, and blistered the cherubim beyond recognition.

Morningstar, now transformed into a horrid dragon, regrouped the fallen cherubim for a counterattack. "Destroy the King!" he shouted as he ordered his forces. "Fly from this place." He waved his mighty wings of skin and scale. With each thrust downward, the Dragon Lord rose up from the white-hot coals. The others followed and so escaped the depths of the abyss, for the way was not yet closed. The intense heat of that place left their flesh a dull red that would never heal. Black stains covered the shards of their tattered robes and armor.

The horde of dragons powered and clawed their way up over the edge of the abyss to the lowlands. Again Morningstar ordered an attack. The rebels flew to the base of the mountain, but no matter how hard they tried, they could not bear the light streaming down from the throne. It repelled them at every try. The King had bound them with chains of gloomy darkness that prevented them from ever entering the realm of the light again.

The defeated rebels fell back to the lowlands. They screamed with anger because of their defeat and pain from their burns. As they observed one another, they despaired over the wretched ugliness that had replaced their beauty. They were no longer cherubs; they were dragons. Every last one.

Morningstar shouted out, rallied his forces, and reasserted his command.

"Do not despair of your wounds, my mighty friends. For darkness is our destiny! Who is to say what is beautiful? Who declares what is right and true? From now on, good is evil and evil is good. Darkness is lovely and the charred blackness of your flesh alluring. You are no longer cherubs enslaved by the King. You are dragons now and I, Morningstar, will lead you to victory. Darkness will spread across the lowlands!"

The dragon horde erupted with snarls and cheers. Then Morningstar called his commanders to his side.

"Lumenon!"

"Yes, my lord. I am here, prepared to fight at your side."

"From this day forward," Morningstar said, addressing the dragon, "you will no longer be called Lumenon. You will be called Darkenor."

The dragons screamed, snarled, and butted their scaly heads against one another in triumph. The rock of the King's mountain echoed back their roar. Creatures across the lowlands turned their heads in the direction of the noise, unaware of the danger invading the calm and harmony of the creation.

"Truly!" Morningstar called out to another of his troops.

"Yes, my lord." Truly answered, and came forward strutting toward Morningstar.

"You will no longer be called Truly. From this day and forever your name is Deceptor."

"Lowly!" Morningstar's right-hand commander snapped to attention, as did all his command.

"You will no longer be called Lowly. From this day forward you will be known as Legion."

Legion saluted Morningstar.

Then Morningstar thrust his featherless wings down with all his strength and rose above the horde.

"I am no longer Morningstar, for I hate the light. From this day and forever you will address me as Lord Dragon."

The dragon horde thundered their approval.

Dragon roots consumed the remaining flesh in their hearts as each bowed to their new master. . . . Snarls and screams, shouts and roars filled the air.

"Evil is glorious." Legion said. The dragons cheered.

"Death to the King." Darkenor said then pumped a fist into the air and shouted, "Long live Lord Dragon."

The dragon horde joined in chanting, "Long live Lord Dragon. Long live Lord Dragon."

The rebels could not return to wage war atop the mountain until they destroyed the light of the throne. For now, they were left to wander the forest lowlands and look for a way to bring their revenge upon the King.

*****

Take heed as you continue, dear reader. For in the following chapters you will start to discern the dragon's tactics against the King's most prized creation: mankind. His twisted schemes are the same today as they have ever been. The father of lies is still whispering to you today. Will you take heed and arm yourself?

Chapter 5

Planning Revenge

Nick stopped for a moment and thought about the warning. What did dragons, seeds, and shadows have to do with his life now? It seemed pretty removed from school, friends, and fights with his mom. But still he wanted to find out what was going to happen next to those crazy dragons.

*****

The dragon horde cursed the King as they traveled through the lowland jungle below the mighty mountain. Their burns crusted over like armor made of scales. Beneath the scales, the searing pain continued to burn for days, but their humiliating defeat angered them more than the pain. Every dragon longed for revenge. Every dragon hated the King.

The dragons painfully moved through the heavy undergrowth. Small creatures climbed above, screeching jungle sounds to announce their position. The dragons marched on, ever fearful of a counterattack from the King's remaining loyal forces. As it was the King's land, they had become trespassers, but in their minds, they felt like conquerors, claiming each acre of ground. They passed creatures of all kinds, silently grazing on the rich plants of the jungle. Some of the beasts were gigantic in comparison to the dragons. They stood as tall as trees, causing fear to rise within the dragons. Several grabbed for their swords, forgetting that all had been lost in battle. Lord Dragon led them onward, seemingly unaffected by the larger creatures. The lesser dragons followed his lead. Their confidence grew as they passed the gentle giants feeding on the leaves of the taller trees.

As they trudged along, the dragons complained to one another. Each had an urgent desire for revenge, but no one had a plan. Lord Dragon, deep in thought, smiled as he listened to their frustrations and complaints. *Revenge will come soon enough*, he thought. While the burning coals robbed him of his former strength and beauty, his mind was as sharp as ever. The lesser dragons observed his silence and guessed that he was formulating a plan. They peppered him with questions, eager to attack again. But the Lord Dragon quieted them, saying it was time to rest for the battle must be won with cunning, not brute strength. Lord Dragon's answer satisfied their curiosity as they marched on.

At last the jungle thinned. The painful slap of branches against their wounds lessened as they dodged the thickets and wove their way along paths made by the giant beasts of the forest. More and more light beamed down through the canopy above until at last they came to a clearing at a shallow river. Halfway across, the Dragon Lord signaled the horde to stop. The cold water soothed their feet. Even so, the dragons preferred the cover of the dense trees. Nervously they scanned the sky above them, fearing a counterattack at any moment. Lord Dragon lifted his gaze as well. Like a wolf sniffing into the wind to locate its prey, he took in a long deep breath.

"There is a garden in this place," he said for all to hear. "I can smell the King's roses."

The dragons shuddered and lifted their eyes toward the skies for fear of attack. Between their growling and snorts, they too could smell the roses. The fragrance they once loved, they now hated. The King they once worshiped, they now cursed in bitter anger.

Lord Dragon, deep in thought, turned toward his forces and shouted for the captain of his guard by name. "Legion!"

Legion, who stood nearby, sloshed through the river to the Dragon Lord and bowed his face. "Yes, Lord Dragon."

"Gather your forces. I wish to address the horde."

"At once."

Legion called the dragons over to the sandy bank on the opposite shore. There they formed a half circle around their commander. Lord Dragon thrust his wings to the ground and rose above the dragons. Charred fragments, the remnants of feathers, fell from his large wings, splashing into the river below.

"The King's forces robbed us of our rightful victory!" He shouted down to the horde gathered on the sand. "The light of the throne threw us backward. Loyalous did not dare meet us alone on the field of battle for a fair fight. Look around, my comrades. We survived and stand strong. Do not fret the loss of your feathers or concern yourself with the burn and scaling of your flesh, for we remain a powerful army. We will have our revenge!"

Lord Dragon's comments excited the dragon throng. The choking black roots within their hearts sent out shoots of revenge and bitterness into the surrounding flesh.

"Snuff out the light of the mountain and victory is ours. Without the light, Loyalous cannot stop us. First we shall rule the lowlands. Then we will conquer the mountain."

The dragon horde shouted their approval. Lord Dragon made great boasts and fooled the company of lesser dragons. If the truth be known, he had no idea how to extinguish the light, yet his ability to deceive and speak half-truths was unmatched. In time he would become known as the *Father of Lies*.

"Do not think we lost the battle," he continued. "It was our destiny to be cast down, for we cannot fight the light of heaven far on top of the mountain. The King tried to destroy us but failed. He is fearful of our strength. He dare not send his forces against us beyond the reach of his light, here in the lowlands. For now we shall gather our strength, living among his creation. Day by day we will infect the whole of it with dragon seed and soon we will rule over all the lowlands." Morningstar shouted again, "We will rule the lowlands!" The dragons roared their approval.

Lord Dragon allowed their response to quiet, then gave his command. "Pull back your forces and remain hidden in the darker jungle. Prepare to scatter if the armies of the King mount a counterattack. Hide in groups of two, prowl the forest quietly like a lion and seek to attack any of their stragglers. Once they're gone, then regroup again. We may be no match without swords in open battle, but we can ambush and crush them one by one. Remember the cherubim are soft—they won't think for themselves as we can. The mindless guardians depend on the King. But we will darken the light of the King and finally destroy them in battle." Again the dragons cheered their commander.

Lord Dragon scanned his surroundings then flew down to the sandy bank where he called in his captains for their orders.

He spoke quietly, "I've heard the King in conversation speak of this place with great delight. Among all of his creation, he loves one creature above the rest. The one he called 'man.' The King made this creature different from all the others. Man is made in the image of the King and has been charged to multiply and fill the lowlands with children and so spread the image of the King to every corner of this land."

With that revelation, the dragon captains gasped. It was a terrifying thought to them.

"We'll see how well this creature called man fares when we sow dragon seed upon his heart." Lord Dragon then tested his lead captain with a short question: "Your orders?"

"We'll be waiting in the darker jungle, my lord," Legion replied.

Then Lord Dragon turned away, sniffed the wind again, and flew toward the fragrance of the roses. The dragon horde pulled back and waited for his return.

*****

"Thanks for coming over to get me. Mom doesn't like it when I leave. But when a friend's waiting for me at the door, what can she say?" Martha sighed as she dropped her heavy backpack onto the floor of her classmate's bedroom and plopped down on the bed. "Things got really tense today, and I thought I was going to explode. I hate their arguing."

"Trouble with Nick again?" Mia asked, sitting down on the floor and leaning her back against a dresser.

"How'd you guess?"

"What did he do this time?"

"He left and didn't tell anyone. My mom was hunting him down most of the morning. Even I started to worry something had happened to him. He must have snuck out last night and then didn't come home. Mom thinks he left early in the morning—she can't bring herself to believe he was out all night. Nick never gets up early on Saturday morning and it's not the first time he's snuck out."

"How do you know?"

"I overheard a couple of his friends talking at school."

"Did they say who he was out with?" Mia looked at her through the corner of her eye as she traced her hand around the strap of her handbag.

"No, I'm guessing it's Tony and some of his friends. Anyway, Mom was a wreck. Nick got in an hour or two before you stopped by to get me. I just hung out upstairs and tried to stay out of it. I can't take it when they fight."

"Well, sounds like a good day to come over here and help me with American Government," Mia said, changing the subject. "I did so bad on that last test. Mom's gonna ground me if I can't pick up my grade. I already think the only reason she's letting me out of the house tonight is because you're here right now helping me study."

"Tonight?" Martha lifted an eyebrow, trying to keep it casual. Ever since she'd skipped a grade last year, she'd still been trying to fit in with her new classmates. She rarely got invited to anything they did. She thought if she started helping Mia study that might get her foot in the door with the older girls. But here again was one more thing she didn't know about.

"Yeah. Stacy, Brooke, and I are all meeting up at Miranda's. That way we can all tell our parents we're doing a sleepover there and we really won't be lying. But the party is three doors down. So that's where we'll be most of the time."

"Party?" Martha couldn't hide her ignorance this time.

Mia rolled her eyes. "Come on, Martha. Everybody knows about Derrick's party tonight," she paused. "But it's probably not something you'd be interested in. You're a little too straitlaced for that." Just then, Mia's phone buzzed from inside her purse. Without looking at it, she casually slid the handbag off her bed.

Martha sat up in the bed and turned toward her friend. "Derrick's house?" She stared at Mia with obvious disapproval.

"What? It's not a big deal," Mia replied.

"It is a big deal. You know what happens at Derrick's house when his parents are gone—everyone knows, even me."

"Oh, come on, it's not like people are getting drunk."

"You sound like you know from experience."

Mia just looked at Martha but didn't answer.

"Admit it. You've already been to one of his parties!" Martha, had suddenly turned into a prosecutor.

"You're just like your mother," Mia shot back.

"My mom? What does she have to do with this?"

"Everything. You know that's why Nick is struggling. Your mom treats him like a kid. He can't do anything on his own."

"He does plenty on his own. That's his problem," Martha said. Thoughts of Nick shouting out disrespectfully against her mom from earlier in the evening flooded her mind. A shadow hovered over her as she thought about how her family had changed since her dad had passed away. But she pushed down her anger. *What good does it do to dwell on the past?* she thought and changed the subject.

"Look, I came over here to get away from the fighting. I came here to help you study, not get into arguments. So do you want to study or not?" she asked.

"Okay, okay, don't get so upset." Mia pulled out their giant government textbook from her backpack. "Memorization. I can't keep all of those crazy dates and facts straight. You said you would show me your secret to acing the test. I'm hoping it involves writing the answers down somewhere."

Mia moved around her bed to the other side of the room and slid a chair out from a petite desk. Martha lifted her backpack off the floor and sat off the side to face Mia. She reached across to her pack, stuck her hand in, and pulled out a stack of index cards.

Mia stole another glance at the phone behind her bag as it sounded off again. She hoped it was far enough away that Martha hadn't noticed. *Mom would hit the roof if she discovered I had another phone*, she thought.

Chapter 6

The Dragon's Temptations

Lord Dragon coursed his way through the thinning jungle on the far side of the river, flying between the thick underbrush and the overhanging branches of large trees. When at last the jungle gave way to open ground, Lord Dragon slowed and landed in one of three tall trees that stood like sentries at the edge of the forest. Down below, animals of every kind were playing together. Off in the distance he could see a vast circular orchard with trees, grapevines, and flowers all planted in neat rows, like spokes of a wheel, streaming out from a central garden court. Tall cliffs protected the orchard on three sides, nestled in a valley at the base of the King's mountain.

While he surveyed the garden, something crashed into the branches below. Lord Dragon looked down to observe a handsome serpent with a stout body, two wings now folded against his body, and a long tail. Shiny scales of blue and green covered the creature with an emerald armor that shimmered in the light.

As Lord Dragon watched, the creature spoke out loud. "I will call you serpent, for you are the wisest of all the creatures in the garden—of all the creatures in the garden, the garden, the garden," he said.

That the creature could speak puzzled Lord Dragon. He knew the king bestowed speech upon the man creatures, created by the King to reflect his image. *But why a serpent?*

"I will call you serpent, for you are the wisest of all the creatures in the garden," the serpent said, repeating the words he'd spoken a moment earlier. Then he spread out two magnificent wings adorned with iridescent feathers that glistened like the scales.

Once again, the serpent repeated himself, "I will call you serpent, for you are the wisest of all the creatures in the garden—of all the creatures in the garden, the garden, the garden."

"Ahh," Lord Dragon whispered as he reasoned. "He only speaks what he hears, he's a repeater." *A perfect host*, he thought. Lord Dragon formed a plan to possess the lesser creature and take over its mind. *Let's see how a creature of the forest fares against the seed of a dragon.* Then he called to the serpent, "What wonderful wings you have," he said, spewing dragon seed. The serpent, startled by the unexpected voice, looked up but said nothing.

Lord Dragon jumped down onto an adjacent branch and did his best to smile as he addressed the smaller creature. "What wonderful wings you have."

"Wonderful wings you have," the serpent said, repeating the compliment as he bowed his head to Lord Dragon.

Lord Dragon spoke again, hoping to get a few dragon seeds to sprout. "You're the wisest creature in the garden."

"You're the wisest creature in the garden," the serpent said and bowed again. He quite enjoyed repeating the sounds of the forest around him.

Lord Dragon grew impatient, confused as to why he couldn't get the dragon seed to grow. It was the serpent's humility that repelled the dragon seed. For just as a seed cannot sprout or grow on solid rock, neither can a dragon seed sprout or grow upon a humble heart.

Lord Dragon thought—then smiled—with another plan. "I am wiser than the king," he said.

The serpent would have been wise not to echo those words, but could not resist the temptation to repeat what he'd heard. "I am wiser than the King," he repeated and again he bowed humbly before the dragon.

Then Lord Dragon stood up tall and proud and roared out with all his strength. "I am wiser than the King!"

The serpent too stood erect and shouted loud for all to hear. "I am wiser than the King!" he said, proudly imitating both the dragon's speech and posture.

At once the dragon seed lying on his heart took hold. The serpent spoke again. "I am wiser than the King." The root of the dragon seed shot down. The serpent, impressed with himself and his ability to mimic the larger dragon, spread his wings and repeated once again, "I am wiser than the King."

Lord Dragon took advantage of the moment. He forced his evil spirit into the serpent down below. The creature shuddered and coughed in a failed attempt to expel the dragon. But it was too late; Lord Dragon possessed him.

The dragon took command of the creature's lesser mind, forced the serpent off his perch against his will, and flew for the center garden courtyard. There he discovered two trees, both heavy laden with fruit. The serpent bent his will against the dragon in an attempt to avoid the tree on the left, but Lord Dragon forced him down to land within its branches. The serpent struggled against Lord Dragon's control but only managed to blurt out a short warning he'd heard earlier that day.

"Do not eat the fruit or you will surely die," the serpent said.

"What is this?" Lord Dragon wondered. Then he encouraged the serpent by repeating what he had heard in the form of a question. "You will surely die?"

The serpent answered, "Of all the trees you may eat, but if you eat of the tree of knowledge of good and evil, you will surely die."

"Ha, ha, ha, ha," Lord Dragon laughed through the serpent's voice. Then he raced about the tree, dusting dragon seed upon every single fruit. "I am the mighty dragon," he said, his voice echoing off the distant mountain. "I am the Dragon Lord!"

Again and again he boasted, spreading dragon seed from top to bottom. "The King should have closed the abyss while he had the chance. Now he will pay. It is just like him to test the loyalty of man. We will see how well he resists my dragon seed."

The serpent, under the dragon's command, shuffled back inside the tree, hiding among the leaves while Lord Dragon's evil mind formed his plan. Birds flitted from tree to tree but not a single one stopped to perch among the branches of the forbidden tree. Off in the distance, a small coney gathered a meal from the fallen fruit. A meerkat joined the coney, pulled a low-hanging grape and munched it happily. From his perch the serpent pitied the small creatures, bound to crawl on all fours for they had no wings.

It wasn't but a few minutes longer before the serpent heard the footsteps of the man and his wife approaching. Just before they passed, he climbed on a higher branch and spread his beautiful wings so that they glistened in the light.

"Now serpent, you should not perch atop the tree of the knowledge of good and evil. It is the forbidden tree," the woman said to the creature.

The serpent smiled, and then Lord Dragon twisted the words of the King as he addressed the woman. "Did the King really say you are not allowed to eat the fruit of any tree?"

"We may eat the fruit of any tree except this tree," the woman said. "For if we even touch it, we will surely die."

"You will not die. The King knows that if you eat this fruit, your eyes will be opened, and you will grow in wisdom like the King, knowing both good and evil."

The serpent climbed further out upon the branch so that his weight lowered the fruit within reach of the woman. She looked at the hanging fruit and took several steps closer—close enough to touch it. The dragon seed blown by the serpent landed upon her heart. As she considered the serpent's words, the dragon seed sprouted.

The fruit looks good enough to eat, she thought. *Why should the king withhold it from us? I can decide for myself what is good for food.*

The man stood nearby but said nothing. Instead of reminding his wife of their earlier warning, he watched as she plucked a single fruit and took a bite.

Without a pause, she turned toward her husband and spoke. "Take and eat it. I'm still alive." She smiled and handed him the bitten fruit.

If she can eat without regret, then so will I, he thought. Then a single seed sown by the dragon cracked open and a tiny root emerged and plunged down where it found the fertile soil of the man's rebellious heart. He could have plucked the dragon seed of pride that sprouted, but chose instead to listen to his wife and also took a bite. That sent the horrid root deeper still.

The sweet pleasure of their pride lasted but a moment, then turned to shame as they looked down upon each other and realized they were naked. The serpent laughed out loud, causing them to run away and hide in a tangle of grapes. For the first time in their lives, they experienced a new emotion.

Shame.

They yanked and pulled at the surrounding vines covered with broad leaves, and wove them together to form something they could use to cover up. Once clothed with the leaves, they felt a little more secure and tried to relax. But not for long. Suddenly they heard the most fearful sound of all—the King's footsteps in the garden.

*****

Nick set the book down and glanced at his phone—no response. While he waited for a reply to his text, he picked up the golf ball and turned it in his fingers. His dad always used the same brand of golf ball, the Ping Eye. Nick never liked the small eye logo printed on the ball. It always seemed to stare up at him. He remembered how his dad would face the eye toward the pin at each tee box. After a few practice swings, he would always say, "See your way to the green."

Nick picked up the phone and texted again to make certain she got his message, then sat back and mused quietly about the last few times he'd been out on the course with his dad. He'd only been eight, barely big enough to swing a full-sized club, but his dad had insisted he "raise him right" and start taking him to play at least twice a month. Out there on the green, time had stopped around them and it was just father teaching son, the two of them soaking in the mid-spring sunshine without a care in the world.

The more the ball rolled around in Nick's hand, the more the questions screamed through his mind.

Dad, why did you have to get cancer? Nick glanced upward. *And why didn't you heal him? Didn't you care about us?*

An angry tear slowly slid down Nick's cheek, the story temporarily forgotten. Up in the ceiling of his bedroom, the watching shadowy figures swirled, churning up the refrain of bitter thoughts and desperate questions that had been hounding him for years.

Chapter 7

The Curse

A warm, savory aroma drifted down the hall and slowly stirred Nick from his dark reverie. Mac and cheese. The familiar comfort food his mom knew he loved.

She made that for me today? After what I did? After how I talked to her?

Something in Nick's heart softened just a bit, warming to the gesture. There was also a twinge of shame.

Sigh. Mom. Well, I'll read one more chapter of this book before I get up to eat. Maybe telling her I read a chunk of this book will smooth things over a little.

*****

Watch the fear the dragon has of the King, dear reader. Though he will never admit it aloud, he now knows the King will always be Lord. He knows with one glance the King can utterly obliterate him forever. Don't be fooled by his massive pride. He is furious because he knows that one day, he will be completely undone. The only hope he has left is to bring down as many of the King's treasured creation with him as he can.

The serpent ducked his head behind a mass of leaves as he watched the King enter the garden court. When the King reached the center of the garden, he called for the man. A pang of fear shot through the serpent as the King approached, glancing down at the half-eaten fruit lying in the grass. The tangled grape leaves rustled when the man turned and stepped out of the shadow of the thicket to answer the King's call. The King then summoned the man and his wife to stand and give an account for their disobedience. The man blamed his wife. She in turn blamed the serpent. The dragon seed roots now embedded in their hearts would not allow them to admit their fault.

The King's voice thundered as he spoke against the serpent. "Because you have done this terrible thing, cursed are you above all the creatures in the lowlands. On your belly you will crawl all your days."

In an instant the serpent's legs shriveled and disappeared. With nothing to grab hold, the creature slipped off his perch through the branches. Instinctively the serpent thrust his arms downward to flap his wings, but they too were gone. So he fell with a thud to the ground next to the woman's feet. The woman stepped back, afraid of the slithering menace.

The King spoke again to the serpent. "I will put enmity between you and the woman and her children. You will bite at her Son's heel, but a future Son will crush your head." The serpent coiled like a spring and lifted his head up into the air ready to strike.

The King turned to the man and woman. The expression on his face turned from fierce anger to sorrow. The man and the woman looked equally sad, now that they knew evil and felt naked and ashamed. The King slid a satchel off his shoulder, thrust his hand inside, and pulled out the skins of two sheep, washed white as snow. He draped the first on Eve, then wiped a tear from her eye, for the King was slow to anger, abounding in steadfast love. "I will greatly increase your pain in childbirth," he said. "You will strive against your husband, but he will rule over you."

Then the King turned to the man and covered him as well. The man understood the cost of the covering. The King had sacrificed two of his prized sheep to provide garments to clothe them. *The King laid the penalty of death upon the sheep instead of upon us*, he thought.

Then the King addressed the man. "Because you listened to the voice of your wife and ate of the tree that I commanded you not to eat, the ground beneath your feet is cursed. The soil will produce thorns when you plant your seed for food and only by hard labor will you grow a crop to eat until the day you return to the ground from which I formed you."

The man and the woman hung their heads as the King's declaration continued. From that day, even until today, every child is born with dragon seed already cast upon the heart, ready to sprout at the first opportunity.

Then the King spoke the saddest words of all. He banished the creatures from the garden. The man and woman could have lived forever, walking in the cool of the garden with the King, eating fruit from the tree of life. To prevent them from ever returning, the King summoned one of his mighty guardians from atop the mountain to guard the valley leading to the garden with a fiery sword. The moment the King lifted his hand to signal, a cherub flew down from the sky above.

The serpent writhed and twisted in agony over the loss of his beautiful wings. Humiliated, he slithered into the leaves to hide and shot away in the taller grass. The man and woman took off running, afraid the serpent might strike them. The cherub drew his flaming sword, ready to slay anyone trying to reenter the garden. He looked forward with his cherubim eyes and watched as the woman and man ran into the forest with the serpent close behind. The woman and the man turned to the right and over a grassy slope, the serpent turned left back into the forest that lead to the darkness of the jungle.

*****

Martha shuffled the index cards a few times then looked up toward Mia. "Before we get started, you've got to promise you won't go tell everybody about my system. Especially when your friends want to know how you got your test scores to improve." She cleared her throat and went on to explain. "Mr. Reynolds adjusts the difficulty of his tests based on the class average scores. We don't need him making the tests more difficult. That might threaten my perfect 4.0."

"You sound confident that I can actually get better grades. Cheating is the only system I know that can do that. Are you sure it's not cheating?"

"Let's call it legal cheating," Martha replied. She knew just how to get Mia interested and didn't let on she heard the earlier buzzing of the phone, which she knew Mia left hidden for a reason. She wanted to know why.

"Legal cheating?" Mia leaned forward. "Now you're talking. What's your secret?"

"First let me see how much you know." Martha pulled a rubber band off the stack of index cards and slipped it onto her wrist. She read the first card. "Question: Which historical documents stipulated that states had the right to nullify federally instituted laws that violated the United States Constitution?"

Mia gave a blank stare as the question hung on the air. Martha motioned with her hand for Mia to answer.

"Well, are you going to give me a few choices?" Mia pleaded.

"No."

"Look, Martha, the tests are always multiple choice."

"You cannot rely on guessing. When you study, you need to challenge yourself to come up with the right answer. That way, you will know the correct answers and won't be so easily fooled by a trick question."

Mia had enough—she didn't have a clue as to the correct answer and guessed that Martha didn't know either. She reached out, grabbed Martha's hands and pinned them down onto the bed to keep her from turning over the card. "Ok, smarty, what's the correct answer?" she asked.

Martha didn't hesitate for a second. "The Virginia and Kentucky resolutions."

Mia yanked the card from Martha's hand, flipped it over, then rolled her eyes. The back read, "The Virginia and Kentucky resolutions."

"Alright, what is the secret? How on earth do you remember all these inane facts?"

"You'll find out soon enough. I first need to see how much you know."

"Let me save you the trouble. I don't know anything. So what is your secret?"

"Ok, I'll tell you, but you have to promise you'll give my system a chance. It does involve a bit of work."

"This had better be cheating. I'm hopeless."

"Do you promise?"

"OK, OK, I promise." Mia said. "What is your secret?"

"I use a mnemonic device that helps you remember facts visually. Rather than try to memorize a list of details, you memorize a silly picture that gives you the answer. Science has proven we remember pictures way easier than we remember data. So I make up a word picture connecting the answers to the questions."

"So you made up a word picture to give you the answer, 'the Virginia and Kentucky resolutions'?"

"Exactly! So for this one I picture this big woman named Virginia running out of her house in her pink lace nightgown with a Kentucky Long Rifle aimed resolutely at a Federal Marshall that trespassed on her farm. She shouts, 'Step foot in my state again and I'll shoot you where it counts and nullify your regulations.' Once I have that silly picture in my head, I never forget it."

"You do that for every question?"

"Every one." Martha smiled and held the stack of index cards up tilting them back and forth in a kind of victory dance. "The sillier the picture, the easier it is to remember."

The phone buzzed again. This time Mia didn't catch herself and glanced over the bed at her purse. She would go along with studying for a while longer. But she had to figure out a way to get Martha out of the room to get to her phone.

Chapter 8

The Spread of the Seed

Once in the darker forest, Lord Dragon withdrew from his possession of the serpent, unsure how the curse upon the serpent would affect him. As soon as he pulled free from the confinement of the creature, he stretched out his arms and wings and smiled wickedly. "Curse the King," he shouted, glad that his own wings escaped judgment. He turned in the direction of the garden and shouted again, "I'll do more than strike against your heel. I will destroy this creation and devour the woman's offspring! Then we will see who rules the mountain."

The serpent slithered off into the grass and never spoke another word. Lord Dragon thrust his wings downward and rose above the underbrush. Then he sped toward the deeper jungle, spewing angry bitter insults as he coursed his way through the increasingly dense maze. It didn't take long for him to approach the horde.

"He's back," Deceptor, the dragon lookout, shouted from his position high up in the trees.

"Lord Dragon returns," another lookout said. "He's alone," he announced.

Moments later the sounds of snorts and snarls echoed.

Snap. Crack. Lord Dragon burst through the thick jungle canopy. Lord Dragon didn't care how much noise he made. His anger toward the King boiled inside of him, ready to explode.

Legion stood and moved to welcome Lord Dragon, bowing at his approach. "Welcome back. We await your orders," he said.

Lord Dragon shouted, "Call a dragon council. Now!"

Legion turned and gave the order, which didn't need to pass through the chain of command, for all the dragons heard the command. The Dragon Lord landed in a small patch of ground, still seething from his encounter with the King. All around him, standing between trees and peering through thick jungle grasses, the dragon horde circled their lord in formation, much as they had once circled the King atop the mountain.

"We have won our first battle," Lord Dragon reported. The dragon horde cheered, yet some of the craftier dragons noted Lord Dragon did not announce that the war was won.

Lord Dragon told the story of the serpent, embellishing the details to impress the victory-starved forces. When he reached the point where he tempted the wife of the man, an excited dragon interrupted, "So what did you think would happen when she reached for the fruit?"

Lord Dragon answered the question, "I expected she would die, and with her any hope that this race of men would multiply."

Several dragons gasped and together blurted in surprise, "She didn't die?" The puzzling news passed dragon to dragon as every dragon down to the last repeated, "She didn't die."

The horde grew silent again, stunned by the revelation and looked to Lord Dragon to explain the apparent miscarriage of justice.

Lord Dragon continued, "Worse still, the serpent took the fall for it all. The King cursed the serpent I possessed, knocking us both to the ground. The creature's magnificent wings and strong legs shriveled and were gone in an instant. My wings, as you can see, were unaffected. As for the man, instead of killing him and his wife, the King poured out his wrath upon two innocent beasts of the field. Then he stripped the fallen animals of their hides. With these skins he clothed the man and woman and forgave their offenses."

The horde stood silent, shocked and confused by the turn of events. Then one lone dragon shouted, "Unjust! The King could not exchange a lesser life for the man," he explained. "It is unjust."

"Unjust!" another shouted as loud as he could.

One by one, the dragons took up the accusation. "Unjust, unjust," they cried till all the dragons chanted, "Unjust, unjust! Unjust!"

"Quiet!" Lord Dragon yelled, silencing the snarling mad dragons with his booming voice. The chanting stopped. The dragons looked to their lord, who said, "It does appear unjust and I do not understand it myself. But there is more to tell. After the curse, the King issued a prophecy that one day the serpent would bite at the heel of a child of man. Though he spoke to the serpent, I believe his word was directed toward me. I would bite at his heel, but the child, the King said, would crush my head. "

Gasps could be heard across the horde. Stunned by the revelation, the dragons pulled back from the circle in fear. Several took cover in the thick foliage. If a man-child could destroy the Dragon Lord, who could stand against mankind? Lord Dragon, sensing their fear, announced his plan.

"Hear me," he called to the group. "Do not fear. No child of man will ever crush my head, for I will do far worse than bite against his heel. We will spread dragon seed across the lowlands. Man will rise up against man and destroy one another. In this way, we will kill the child! Destroy the child and you destroy the promise. Destroy the promise and you destroy the King's perfection, and then the light of the mountain turns to shadow. We will rule over all!"

"We are an invincible army!" he shouted. Then he led them in repeating his promise, chanting one word at a time, "We! Will! Rule! Over! All!"

The Dragon Lord spread his wings, lifted his hands, and repeated, "We! Will! Rule! Over! All!"

The dragons rose up from the shadows and joined in the chorus. "We! Will! Rule! Over! All! We! Will! Rule! Over! All!" rang out through the forest.

When at last the horde grew quiet, Lord Dragon gave each their instructions. Then he scattered his forces across the lowlands to practice their evil ways upon the lesser creatures of the earth. The dragons were spirit creatures, whose bodies were most often invisible to the other animals of the land. They also had the ability to possess a lesser creature and speak through them. The stronger dragons, though normally unseen by humans, could show themselves for short periods of time. But without the light of heaven to strengthen them, the dragons were weak and had no physical power over man. Still, their dragon seed was a deadly poison and their greatest weapon.

*****

What follows next, dear reader, is a vital retelling of history. See the dragon's schemes. Understand his movement through the centuries, the millennia. Humans were always his target. It was then, and it is now. It started in the garden, but it continued through floods, prophets, and kings. Not only did he seek to drag away as many members of the human race as possible, but he knew there was a promised Child coming. It brought a chill to his very bones. Someone who threatened the very heart of his seething rebellion.

*****

In the course of time, the man and his wife gave birth to a son. The dragons referred to him as the "firstborn" and bent all their evil forces against him. Soon the prideful roots he inherited from his father's seed began to grow. The dragon horde spewed fresh seed upon him that also found the fertile soil of his prideful heart. It too sprouted and sent down more roots.

Then a second, far humbler, child was born to man. He resisted prideful thoughts and fought against the dragon seed. He loved the stories of the King his father passed down. The garden of old seemed glorious, and he longed to walk side by side with the King as his father once did. His father didn't hide his failure and warned him of the deadly dragon seed. While the firstborn son ignored his father's counsel, the second born began to worship the King, offering sacrifices from the best of his flock.

The dragons, fearing the younger son was the child of promise foretold in the prophecy, turned the heart of the firstborn against his younger brother. The older brother became so jealous that he murdered his younger brother in an angry rage. The dragons celebrated their victory that night, praising their Lord Dragon and his brilliant plan.

But over time, the woman gave birth to many more children, and they in turn married and bore children of their own. Lord Dragon, in an effort to tempt the growing numbers of men, spread his forces thin across the land, sowing fresh dragon seed into their hearts wherever possible. With a goal to wipe any memory of the King from their minds, the Dragon Lord nearly succeeded. His evil infection spread until only one family remained loyal to the King.

The King regretted his creation and could not overlook the evil rebellion of his creation any longer. For he saw that every inclination of the thoughts of the human heart were only evil all the time. To bring judgment and purify the land of evil, the King opened the floodgates of the heavens and the great fountains of the earth, submerging the whole world below and destroying all life on the earth.

The dragons celebrated as they watched the lowlands scoured by the flood. They laughed, giddy with the victory, until they caught sight of a ship floating upon the waves, riding out the storm. The King did not allow his promise to die, for his word is always true.

So there upon the waves one loyal family rode out the storm of judgment brought by the king across the lowlands.

The dragons cried foul and tried to get inside the vessel to spread their evil seed, but the doors were shut tight. They searched tirelessly for a weakness, but the King himself designed the vessel and sent guardians to watch over it. It took months for the water to recede once the skies turned blue. The dragons traveled to and fro across the lowlands biding their time.

Within days after the waters retreated and humans set foot upon the earth, the dragons were back spreading their evil dragon seed. Once again the hearts of even this loyal family became corrupted by the deadly seed, but with each generation, the King poured blessings and grace to preserve a remnant to carry forth the knowledge and hope of his promise. Their offspring multiplied and scattered for thousands of miles in every direction.

Lord Dragon and his dragon horde spread themselves thin, convincing many that there never was a King at all. And while most forgot about the King, those that settled closest to the mountain kept his memory alive. Now and again the King visited his people. At other times he sent his guardians to watch over them. These interactions encouraged their faithful loyalty to the King.

After a thousand years and more of spreading dragon seed, the Dragon Lord came to realize there was only one path to victory. The number of people over the lowlands were once again too great. He must go after the child. The Lord Dragon listened to the King's prophets for information and clues. Their prophecies, meant to encourage the people of the land, contained information the ruler of the dragons intended to use to his advantage.

Once Lord Dragon found the evidence he sought, he sent word through Legion to call a council of the dragon horde. After piecing together hidden clues extracted from a rebel scribe, he believed the promised child would soon be born in one of the cities nestled near the base of the mountain.

Chapter 9

The Prophecy

As time passed, the lesser dragons did all they could to spread their evil seed among the lowland clans. They corrupted the poorest of men and the greatest of kings. Even the wisest king to ever live fell prey to the temptations whispered by the dragons and foolishly rejected the King of the Mountain. While the seeds of pride sown by the dragons destroyed whole nations, there was always a remnant of faithful folk who loved the King and refused to turn away from him.

The dragons trained their eyes upon each succeeding generation for any sign of the biggest threat of all—the Prince. They listened to the many prophecies for clues and watched for any sign of his coming. So when their seed corrupted a key scribe, who knew well the prophecies and signs, the Dragon horde commanded he tell them all. The scribe, whose hatred grew against the King was only too happy to oblige.

Until finally . . .

"The time has come!" Lord Dragon shouted to the horde.

"We've scoured the land for the promised child without success. Up till now we've been guessing blindly. But no more. Pay attention, my friends." Lord Dragon shouted, "Bring in the scribe."

Out from the darkness of the surrounding wilderness, a frail old man appeared hunched over, his robes ragged and torn. He held a scroll under his arm.

Lord Dragon looked down at the approaching man, who cowered in fear as he drew near the ominous shadowy dragon. The Dragon Lord ushered his command. "Open the scroll," he commanded.

The scribe wasted no time obeying. He unrolled the scroll on the ground in the center of the dragons and held it open with two rocks at either end. Gold leaf and colorful filigree designs decorated the text. Once the scroll was fully open, the man looked up and spoke.

"Have you ever seen a more beautiful scroll? I think not," he said, answering his own question as he admired his handiwork. "I worked as a scribe, charged to copy the ancient prophecies. My scrolls were the most beautiful of all. Everyone admired my work and celebrated their beauty. But when upon this scroll I made a simple copy error, the lead scribe ordered it destroyed. For by the King's edict, no mistakes could ever be allowed. If the truth were known, I did not make a mistake; I added my signature to the line of the scroll. The words I copied were perfect. Six letters more, that spelled out my name. I knew that future scribes would copy it forever after me. My name would live on!"

The dragons howled to hear him boast. They could see how the scribe was consumed with dragon seed. The man could not resist and was theirs to command.

"Show us the prophecy," the Dragon Lord commanded.

The scribe slapped his palm down upon the scroll and pointed to a line. "Hear now the prophecy of the King," he said with a deep, sober tone of voice that caused the dragons to shrink back in fear. It was the word prophecy that caused them to shiver, for the dragons knew the King's prophecies always came true and they worried what the scribe would reveal. The man pointed to a line of the scroll and translated one word at a time as he read:

The lowlanders who walked in darkness have seen a great light;
those who dwelt in a forest of deep darkness,
on them light of the mountain has shone.

The word *light* concerned the dragon horde, but the rest of the prophecy simply terrified them.

For to the lowlanders a child is born,
a son is given as a gift;
and the government of all the land below the mountain
shall be upon his shoulders,
and he will be called
Wonderful, Mighty,
Everlasting Father, Prince of Peace.

There will be no end to his rule
And he will sit upon the throne of his fathers
From now and for all eternity.
The zeal of the King of the Mountain will do this.

The dragon horde shrunk back, silenced by the prophecy. The lesser dragons didn't understand all the meaning, but even they were clever enough to know that it was terrible news.

Lord Dragon thrust down his wings and rose high over the horde to begin his address. "Do not be concerned or think this prophecy will stand. The King has made a grave mistake in speaking his plan through the prophets. Now that we have this word, we will use it against him for our own advantage to victory."

The dragon horde listened attentively to their leader speak but remained unconvinced that victory was anywhere close at hand.

Lord Dragon continued, hoping to rekindle enthusiasm within the dragon ranks. "In our efforts to exact revenge upon the throne, we've lost our focus. We have become distracted with trying to destroy the entire race of human men when we need to kill only one child!"

Killing one child was easy, but which child—that one thought filled the minds of the dragons.

"This is the meaning of the prophecy: It says 'a Son to be born' who the prophets called both 'Father' and 'Prince of Peace.' Listen carefully. The King plans to send his very own Son, the Prince, into the lowlands as a man. Hear what I say. If we kill the King's Son, we destroy the King, and his Spirit forever dies, for the King, the Prince, and the Spirit are inseparably linked as one."

"We thought our battle was against the King atop the mountain, but once the Son is born, our battle will be fought here, in the lowlands. You will be my scouts. We will sow the dragon seeds of pride across the land; and when the Prince is born as a man child, we will destroy him. The prophecy will be broken, and the light of heaven will turn dark."

The Dragon Lord's explanation excited the horde and fed their desire for revenge. Their shouts of approval grew louder.

Lord Dragon raised his voice above the growing clamor and shouted. "Then we will rule the world from that time forth and forevermore. That is *my* prophecy!"

The dragon horde shouted their approval.

Lord Dragon held up his hands to silence their celebration and spoke out again, "We need not scour all the far-off cities and lands, for the prophecy is clear. The Prince will sit upon the throne of kings of old. That means he will be born in the royal line of the kings of man. While there are many tribes across the lowlands, the royal clan is not so large and built their cities in a pocket of land at the base of the mountain."

"What is more, I believe the King will send the Prince into the lowlands with proper recognition. As sure as I stand before you, the Prince will be born to royal fanfare somewhere in a palace. So, my dragons, fly at once and guard the palace and every royal home.

Sow your seed among the scribes and religious rulers of the land. When you discover the royal babe, get word back to me and I will crush his head."

The dragons howled at the thought and beat their fists upon their chests. Knowing the prophecy ahead of time was key. Soon they would destroy the child, then they would rule the mountain.

Caught up in their celebration and intoxicated by their pride, not a single dragon noticed the bright light that flashed in the western sky above the fields surrounding the City of the Giant Slayer.

*****

Nick paused his reading for a moment, surprised at how long it had pulled him in. By now the smell of mac and cheese was overpowering and he rose to cautiously head down to the kitchen, stomach growling.

*****

Ok, one last question and we can be finished studying," Martha said flipping up the final card. "See if you can get it. QUESTION: What do you call a prolonged speech designed to delay an action in the senate, often referred to as rule 22?"

"I know, I know," Mia shouted, waving her hand in the air. "Wait, give me a minute to remember the picture. Philip was so glad to see Nate that he talked and talked with him as the bus turned down route 22. The answer–Phil-bus turned–filibuster! The answer is filibuster!"

"Good. Where do they use a filibuster?" Martha further questioned Mia.

"So glad to see Nate! See Nate—Senate! They use the filibuster in the Senate!" Mia shouted again.

"What does a filibuster involve?"

"Talk and talk and talk." She couldn't believe she was getting the answers to the questions correct.

"Great job, Mia! See how easy it is to remember a word picture?" Martha leaned back triumphantly. Mia seemed to really be enjoying her company while they studied. Maybe she wasn't hiding the content of the text, perhaps she was afraid to let on she had a phone. But Martha wanted to know for sure—and she had a plan. "Let's stop for now," Martha suggested. "I know I need a break. Is your restroom just down the hall safe?"

"I'd use the downstairs bathroom," Mia answered quickly, seeing her chance to get Martha out of the way for a few minutes. Sending her down to the bathroom would give her time to check her phone, which had buzzed several times while they worked their way through the thick stack of flashcards. "My brothers use the one up here. It's not safe."

"Ok, thanks for the warning. I'll go downstairs."

Martha stood up, opened the bedroom door and walked into the hall. But instead of walking downstairs, she waited by the closed door. After a moment, she heard Mia's phone buzz again.

Perfect, Martha thought. In a moment she would be able to find out what was really going on.

Chapter 10

The Arrival of the Maharajahs

After sending still another text, Nick shuffled into the kitchen, glancing around for his mom or grandma. It seemed they were somewhere else in the house. On the stovetop sat a pan full of steaming mac and cheese. Next to it on the counter were a bowl and a note.

> "Thought you might enjoy your favorite lunch this afternoon. Didn't want to bother you in case you were busy reading the book I gave you. Go ahead and take a bowl back to your room if you'd like. A treat for the day. I'm out reading on the back deck. Feel free to come see me anytime you want."

Whoa. What had gotten into Mom? Nick was never allowed to eat in his room. *And the mac and cheese wasn't bait to get him into the same room to talk with her again? Man, she must really want him to pay attention to that book.*

Part of Nick's heart wanted to lash back, refusing to go back to the leather-bound volume on his bed. If she wanted him to do it that badly, there must be some trick up her sleeve. And wasn't he trying to prove to her that he was his own boss?

Just meet her halfway, a thought suddenly whispered itself into his heart. Hidden above him, Bitterlous and Arrogance shrieked at the shaft of light that suddenly shone through the kitchen window.

It's your life! Your life! they hissed in his ear. *Don't be a mama's boy!* they implored, concerned that the beam of light threatened their work.

The invisible guardian who entered the room with the light reasoned truthfully against the council of the shadows. *She's not even forcing you to talk to her about it. It's just a gift she wants you to have.*

The dragons raged all the more as Nick stood in thought for a minute, then finally picked up the bowl and headed back to his room.

*****

The time for the fulfillment of the promise had come. Within a day's journey of the wilderness, angelic praise thundered down from the heavens, and the bright light of the guardians filled the sky. A group of shepherds watching over their flocks outside the City of the Giant Slayer cowered in fear and amazement at the sight. It was to this group of humble shepherds that the guardians delivered the greatest birth announcement of all time.

Following the directions given by the guardians, the shepherds left their sheep asleep on the hillside to search for the child born in a cattle stall. These humble, affectionate hearts became the first earthly worshipers of the One who had come to rescue the lowlanders from the curse of the dragon.

Meanwhile the dragons missed this momentous day. Searching for a royal prince, they totally missed the humble birth. So for now, the infant prince slept in peace. Had Lord Dragon discovered the nature of the birth in advance, it is doubtful he would have believed the Prince who lived in glorious light atop the mountain could ever be born in a stable. With the dragons searching in all the wrong places, the Prince was safe, at least for now.

*****

As the child passed his first birthday, the prophecies of the child drew the interest and affections of a company of wise men whose hearts yearned for a Savior. A sign in the heavens, a bright star in the night sky, led these three Maharajahs through the desert sands toward the child. These earnest astrologers, leading an opulent caravan from the East, marched their camels, bronze bells clanging from highly decorated saddles, across the wilderness, not far from where the dragons gathered. But the dragons, tired by their search for the child were asleep without a single sentry posted to observe the royal procession.

The Maharajahs never saw the twisted shadows of the dragon horde scattered upon the sand, for they fixed their gaze upon the star. They believed it would lead them to the Prince, who was now only months away from his second birthday. They planned to worship him, and came bearing gifts of gold, frankincense, and myrrh.

Not long after the last camel disappeared over the horizon, Lord Dragon awoke, panicked by a terrible dream within which he saw the King cast him and the other dragons into the abyss. His nightmare reignited Lord Dragon's bitter anger toward the King and renewed his passion to target the promised child. Lord Dragon stood tall, spread his wings wide, and let off a bone-chilling scream that echoed through the wilderness. When he looked down at the sleeping horde, his blood boiled.

"Wake up, you lizards!" Lord Dragon said as he kicked his two commanders, Legion and Deceptor.

Legion jumped to his feet, using his wings to shield his face from the brilliance of the morning sun. "What are your orders, my lord?" he asked, bowing to his commander.

"Get this rabble up. We've got a royal child to murder."

"Yes, my lord, I will wake the forces. But what shall I tell them are the orders of the day? They've grown tired of the search."

"Silence! The mission has not changed. We search for the child. We will find him. I sense within my being he's arrived."

"How shall we recognize him?" Legion asked, hoping the Dragon Lord could give him something to pass along to his forces.

"You can be sure of one thing," Lord Dragon offered. "You'll know him when you see him. The glory of the King's Son will be easy to recognize among the common people. Remember, if we kill the Prince, we kill the King. Now wake this rabble."

Legion called his commanders and woke the forces, passing along the same urgency. Within minutes the dragon horde stood at attention. The Dragon Lord shared the day's plan.

"DeJealous and I will go straight to the Temple City and visit again with the reigning monarch. He too is hungry for power and ready to destroy any threat to his claim on the throne. Perhaps he will have news of the Prince. If so, we will incite jealousy in him that we can use to our advantage. As soon as any of you hear anything, report back to me in the Temple City. Commanders, scatter your forces."

With one thrust of his wings downward Lord Dragon rose to the sky, and DeJealous followed. The commanders below barked orders through the torrent of dust and sand. In a moment their leader flew out of sight. The three-day journey to the temple city over the dunes took Lord Dragon but an hour. He passed over the Maharajahs' caravan just before reaching his destination. The caravan below proceeded on toward the city, safely undisturbed by the dragons passing overhead.

"We shall arrive in the city within the hour," said the taller of the Maharajahs, who had traveled all the way from Sheba. As he spoke, the dragon passed above.

"Once there, we must seek an audience with the king and ask if he has seen the child," said the second of the Maharajah, who was Arabian.

"Are we certain we're headed in the right direction?" asked the third, a Midianite. "I'm more certain at night when we can follow the star."

The Arabian spoke. "The star pointed us toward the Temple City, and there is little else of significance around. I'm certain we'll find the promised son within its walls."

"A star shall rise in the land of the Temple City," the Maharajah from Sheba said, quoting the prophecy. "We're headed in the right direction. I just don't know if he is within these walls, or perhaps beyond."

The Maharajahs made their way through the main gate, a large opening in a massive wall of stone. Word spread through the streets of their arrival. When they reached the palace, the king granted the three travelers an audience. The king's stewards ushered them into the vestibule of the throne room to wait. Meanwhile, the king of the Temple City adorned himself with jewels, preparing to meet with his guests. Lord Dragon, who arrived a moment earlier, didn't waste any time. He stood in the royal chambers invisible from view, whispering a nonstop barrage of praise, ever sowing dragon seed upon the heart of the king. As soon the fresh seed found the soil of his heart, it sprouted and sent its blackened roots deep.

*****

With Martha gone, Mia reached across the bed for her backpack, pulled out her phone, put in her passcode, and started to read her texts. Moving her fingers as fast as she could, she replied.

Just as she pushed "send," Martha burst through the door.

Mia jumped. Martha's sudden entry scared the daylights out of her. "What are you doing scaring me?" Mia protested but tried not to raise her voice.

Martha peered over Mia's shoulder. "Who are you texting?" she asked.

Mia refused to answer, so Martha grabbed the phone. "Let go of my phone," Mia demanded as she struggled to pull the phone back out of Martha's hand. Martha held the phone close to her chest.

"Give it back to me!" Mia shouted. But Martha pulled it away, out of Mia's reach, long enough to read the whole message string. She expected to see a text from Derrick. So, when she saw that the texts were actually from her brother Nick, she yanked herself away from Mia and said, "What on earth are you doing texting my brother?"

Mia suddenly calmed down and whispered, "Not so loud." She pushed Martha aside and closed the bedroom door, so her mom wouldn't hear the conversation.

"What are you doing texting my brother?" Martha repeated.

"It's none of your business. Give me my phone."

"Text him back and tell him you can't go, or I am going down into your kitchen and telling your mom about the phone."

"Martha! If she catches me with another phone—well, let's just say I'll get all the study time I need. Come on, Martha. We are only friends."

"Since when do 'only friends' sneak out to go to parties?"

"I didn't go with him last night. He was with the guys. Honest, this is the first party I even got invited to. I swear."

"Text him." Martha held out the phone. Mia had no choice and Martha knew it.

Mia grabbed the phone and texted, "can't go after all, u r on your own." She pressed send, then handed the phone back to Martha.

Martha texted a second message.

"What are you saying?"

"Just making sure the message is clear," Martha replied.

"What did you say? If you don't tell me and give me back my phone, I'll tell everyone about your secret system."

"Go ahead, if they start using it and get better grades, the tests will only get harder. I'll do fine, but what will you do?"

Martha popped open the back of the phone and pulled out the battery. "You won't be needing this." She threw the phone back on the bed, "There's your phone back. If I find out you're calling or texting Nick again, I'll tell your mom about your phone. For now, it will just be our little secret."

Martha picked up her backpack and tossed her index cards back inside after pulling the rubber band from her wrist onto the stack. Then she said, "I'd better go."

"You aren't going to tell my mom about the phone, right?"

"I told you, only if you don't leave my brother alone." Martha walked past Mia and opened the door. Mia followed behind.

Chapter 11

To the City of the Giant Slayer

After washing his face and combing his beard, the King of the Temple City slipped on his royal robes and prepared to meet the Maharajahs. He traveled down a marble-lined corridor, which led to the throne room where he passed through a curtain doorway. There before him stood his marble throne. A simple floral design layered with gold leaf adorned the massive stone. The king settled slowly into his regal seat, then adjusted the folds of his garment before motioning to the guard.

"Bring them in," he directed. Then he signaled for a minstrel to play. The musician plucked the strings of his cithara, instantly filling the hall with music. The delightful melodies combined with the fragrance of fresh cinnamon oil wafting from six lamps burning in the hall. The servants had moments ago sprinkled the oil upon the hot lamps, filling the room with the sweet aroma.

The guard opened an iron-studded door that led into the vestibule. While the king waited patiently, he wondered if the Maharajahs might offer him a gift. When all three had fully entered the room, he greeted them with great respect.

"Welcome, honored travelers! You must be tired from your journey through the desert. What brings you to the Temple City?"

"Your hospitality is unmatched, great king, and your welcome and this audience greatly appreciated," the Arabian said while another of the Maharajahs approached the king and bowed, waiting for the King's approval.

"You may rise," the king ordered, then motioned the man to advance. The Maharaja passed a silken satchel to the king, who opened it immediately. He turned the sack upside down and a string of weighty pearls dropped into his open palm.

"A kingly gift of unmatched quality," the monarch said to acknowledge the present.

"Oh, good king, we have come to find the prince foretold of long ago. The prophets say he is to be sent by the King of the Mountain to be born among men. We followed his star by night to your city and have come to worship him and bring him gifts," the Arabian said, introducing the reason for their visit. "We are hoping you would be able to tell us of his whereabouts."

Lord Dragon pushed DeJealous forward, who specialized in inciting rivalry, jealousy, and envy. His snakelike tongue whispered from the shadows into the king's ear. "A rival Prince will steal your throne if you allow him to survive. You must find him."

Still, the king reasoned, he had not heard of such a king. Perhaps the Maharajahs were mistaken. He decided to check with his counselors who studied the prophetic writings of old.

"I have not heard of such a Prince," the king replied evenly, careful not to show any emotion. "But let me gather my counselors and call upon their knowledge and wisdom. Perhaps they've heard news of a royal child or can discern the place of his birth from the ancient writings. In the meantime, I insist you remain as my guests. You shall rest, feast, and refresh yourselves until I call."

The Maharajahs, glad for the opportunity to rest, agreed.

When the counselors arrived, the king of the Temple City anxiously inquired if they knew of such a Prince, sent from the King of the Mountain. "Surely it is a wild tale they have concocted to test the strength of my kingdom!"

"There is such a prophecy, my lord. It tells of a future Prince to be born in the line of the kings of old—born in the City of the Giant Slayer," they said.

The king shrunk back as his fears were confirmed. DeJealous, carefully fanning his rage and pride, jumped at the opportunity and whispered again into his ear. "You can use the Maharajahs to your advantage. Send them off to locate the child. No need to give up the advantage of a surprise attack by sending a large force of troops. Once you know the whereabouts of the child, you can send a single assassin to eliminate the threat."

Lord Dragon admired the cunning strategy of DeJealous and congratulated himself for bringing him along.

The king smiled at the thought of using the Maharajahs to track down the child. If he flattered their wisdom and character enough, they would be all too eager to send back word so that he too could pay homage to the King. *Yes, that will work brilliantly*, he thought, commending himself for the ingenious plan.

The king sat again upon his throne and summoned the Maharajahs. When they returned, refreshed from their rest, he inquired as to what time they first observed the star.

"The star appeared in the sky nearly twenty months ago," offered the Arabian.

Then the king shared the prophecy his counselors had revealed to him and directed the Maharajahs to resume their search in the City of the Giant Slayer, where he was convinced they would find the prince.

"When you have found the royal child," he said, "please bring me word that I too may come and worship him."

The Maharajahs rejoiced in the news. They excitedly pulled out their maps and confirmed that the City of the Giant Slayer stood in line with the star's trajectory. Grateful for his help, they agreed to send the King word of the child's whereabouts. The Maharajah thanked the King and withdrew from his presence. As soon as they left the king's audience, the seasoned astrologers determined to set out that very same night.

They ordered their servants to load the camels and prepare for the six-mile journey. By the time the servants completed the task, the first of the stars flickered in the darkening sky. The king of the Temple City, not expecting his regal guests to travel by night, assigned no guard to watch them. Lord Dragon was similarly fooled. The Maharajah's servants, hoping to avoid disturbing the king's sleep, held noise to a minimum as they assembled the caravan.

The light of day surrendered to dusk as the last camel sauntered into line. The Maharajahs mounted their dromedaries and signaled the column to move. Within minutes the star appeared again in the sky before them. When they beheld the sign, they rejoiced, for it rose toward the City of the Giant Slayer, again confirming the word given by the King's advisors. The star led them out of the Temple City, and after a short journey, they arrived at the City of the Giant Slayer. Still following the star, they moved quietly through the heart of the town, then down an unassuming street to a single home, where the light of the star beamed through the darkness to shine on one doorway.

The Maharajahs dismounted. The jangle of buckles and a soft groan from the camels echoed in the quiet of the night. The travelers secured their gifts, then knocked upon the wooden door. A young woman opened the beautifully carved olivewood slab and stepped out toward them. She held a young boy in her arms and welcomed the Maharajahs into her home. At that moment, the star burst forth with an even brighter ray of light, which illuminated the child in her arms. The wise and weary sojourners bowed, convinced they were in the presence of the Prince himself. The young woman smiled and scanned their astounding caravan, then turned into the room for her guests to follow. Once inside, the Maharajahs bowed again in worship and offered gifts of myrrh, frankincense, and gold.

As the travelers presented their gifts, a deep delight filled their hearts. The child's parents shared all that had transpired with the birth of their son. They spoke of the visit of a mighty cherub, who announced that the Prince would be given by the Spirit of the King—born to the woman, but not of the curse of man. Because their son was conceived by the Spirit of the heavenly King and not the flesh of man, he lived untainted by the curse. Not since the creation of the first man and woman had a child been born who was free of the evil dragon roots of pride.

Glad for their visit and filled with an incredible joy, the Maharajahs soon said farewell and took leave of the humble home. After re-forming the caravan, they exited the narrow space between the surrounding houses. The clop of the camels' feet faded as they made their way through the city and out the main gate. Once outside the town, the company halted for the night and hoisted tents in an open field. The next morning, they set out at dawn. Having been warned in a dream not to return to the Temple City, they turned toward home and departed by a different route.

When the King of the Temple city awoke to find the travelers gone, he ordered an investigation to discover their whereabouts. Merchants who were just arriving reported passing their caravan early that morning well beyond the walls. When news of their departure reached the king of the Temple City, he realized the Maharajahs had tricked him. He screamed and ran through the palace, throwing over the furnishings. Dragon seed roots of bitter jealousy gripped his soul. The servants hid at the sound of the crashing. They were familiar with the king's rampages and dared not stand in his way.

But the king's distress could not be compared to the rage the Lord Dragon displayed. His roar echoed through the palace sending tremors through the stone walls. Lord Dragon shouted, "We cannot be deceived! We must devour the child."

The king answered the call to arms and, being a mere puppet of the dragon, sprang into action and shouted "Captain!"

Within moments everyone in the palace court heard the king shout the gruesome order. "Go at once to the City of the Giant Slayer with a full battalion. Seize every young boy, two years old or younger, and put them to the sword. Search the city and the surrounding country. Kill the children and anyone who stands in your way."

But like the Maharajahs, the parents of the Prince were also warned in a dream and had made their escape by the time the soldiers arrived. Following the directions they received, they moved to a foreign land far from the reach of the evil king. There they lived in peace and safety with plenty of gold, thanks to the Maharajahs, to care for their son's every need. It seemed to them that the King of the Mountain had planned it all.

Back in the Temple City, the evil king boasted all the more, certain his raid had succeeded. But Lord Dragon wasn't as sure. He feared that the Prince had escaped. He could sense it in his dragon bones. And when he dared look up to the sky, the light of the mountain radiated across the lowlands. Somewhere in the land, the Prince was still alive and well.

And the Lord Dragon was determined to find him.

Chapter 12

The Prince Is Discovered

Convinced the puppet King of the Temple City had failed him, Lord Dragon gathered the horde and ordered his own army to scour the City of the Giant Slayer and its surrounding lands in an effort to find the royal child. Week after week, year after year they searched, and still the light shown down from atop the Mountain of the King. The dragons were so intent on finding a regal prince that several of the dragons passed by the young Prince while he played in the dusty streets with the other children. The dragons could not fathom that the King's Son would be born as an ordinary man to a carpenter and his wife.

Beyond missing the Prince who grew up right under their noses, the dragons also failed to understand the key to breaking the curse. The Prince must fulfill three requirements. First, since only humility could break the hold of dragon seeds upon a heart, the Prince must lay aside his glory and be born in humility as a mortal man. Second, he then must personally face the Dragon Lord and resist his alluring temptations, not allowing a single seed to sprout.

Finally, after living to adulthood, the Prince must be punished to pay the penalty for the pride of man. He must be cursed by the King in place of man and die as man's substitute. His victory over pride and the resulting curse would come through a humiliating death. The King so loved the lowlanders that he asked his only Son, the Prince, to leave his throne and take upon himself this sacrificial mission.

Though the Prince had lived forever as the Son of the heavenly King, he did not hold tightly to that royal claim. At the King's request, the Son laid aside his glory and took on the frailty of man. The arrogant dragons hadn't a clue.

So year after year, Lord Dragon and all his forces searched in vain. Their repeated failure to discover the Prince angered the Dragon Lord. The angrier he became, the more he ordered his forces to attack the lowlanders and turn them all against the King.

Lord Dragon sent his dragon forces to possess as many young men as they could. The more idolatry and corruption he incited, the more he appeased the bitter anger he held toward the King. The men and women possessed by the horde served as human spies, ever listening for clues that might lead the dragons to the Prince. It was one of these spies that first uncovered the secret identity of the King's Son—now the full-grown son of a carpenter. The dragon who possessed the spy, named Prowler, reported back to Lord Dragon, eager to receive credit for his most spectacular discovery.

"I possessed a village boy and lead him to thievery," Prowler began recounting the story. He was so proud of his accomplishment that he bounced with excitement as he spoke. "Some of the villagers took the lad to the wilderness hoping that the boy might hear the words of a prophet who could perhaps cast me out. It was in listening to this prophet that I discovered the secret identity of the Prince," Prowler explained.

"How do you know he was a true prophet?" Lord Dragon inquired. "There have been no prophets for four hundred years—since the last of the writings were recorded."

"He wore camel hair like the prophets of old and called to the masses to repent of their pride. He claims to speak for the King."

Lord Dragon accepted the explanation. While the prophets had been silent for several hundred years, it would make sense for a prophet to announce the coming of the Prince. "So what about the Prince?" Lord Dragon demanded.

"The prophet pointed to a common man, the son of a carpenter, and called him a Lamb. He then declared the carpenter would be the one to destroy the curse or something like that," Prowler said.

"What do you mean 'something like that'? You bring me riddles. We've been searching for thirty years. I'm looking for a Prince, not a Lamb!" Lord Dragon shouted as he paced back and forth. "I send out an army of dragons and this is what you bring me—a carpenter's son? Do you think I am a fool?"

"He is the Prince," Prowler said in his defense. "I would have dismissed him too if not for hearing the voice of the King himself confirm it. Even the Spirit appeared as a dove to hover over his head." The lesser dragon braced for another angry reply, for he knew the story was difficult to believe. But the pieces were coming together for the Dragon Lord.

"Curse him!" Lord Dragon pounded his fist into his open hand.

Prowler flinched, then eased when Lord Dragon commended him.

"Well done. You are not as worthless as I first thought."

He paced again and then turned. "So the Prince has been hidden as a common woodworker?"

"Yes, my lord."

"Strange. And now you say the King has announced his Son? I wonder why? Why announce him now?"

"I don't know."

"Think, you fool! There must be a reason." Lord Dragon sauntered away, talking to himself as he did. "Hide him from us while he is young and vulnerable, then announce him to the world when he is strong so he can set up his throne here." Lord Dragon turned again to face Prowler. "How was he dressed? As a prince with the finest silk and golden embroidery?"

"He was dressed as a common man. He wore a simple tunic." Prowler shrunk back, fearing another explosive reaction.

"A simple tunic? That makes no sense. Did he wear a crown or signet ring or hold a staff?"

"None that I saw. He dressed more like a shepherd than a king."

"Now I've heard it all. I'm looking for a Prince and you bring me news of a carpenter dressed like a shepherd. Do you think I have time for this nonsense?"

"But I heard the King affirm his Son," Prowler appealed.

"You say you heard the voice of the King. What did the King say?"

"His words were short but unmistakable. 'This is my beloved Son in whom I am well pleased,'" Prowler answered.

As soon as Lord Dragon heard the familiar title "beloved Son," he knew that Prowler had found the Prince. The details confused him but he remembered from his service atop the mountain hearing the King often call the Prince his beloved Son. *Time is critical*, he thought. With a renewed urgency, he questioned the lesser dragon. "Where did this carpenter go?"

"I followed him into the wilderness. He took no food; he traveled straight into the wasteland. I followed at a distance for days until I was certain of his path, and then I set out searching for you."

"Days!" Lord Dragon shouted. "How long has it been since you left him?" Lord Dragon swung his arms about in disbelief. "Days? I am to be notified immediately and you come at me with some sorry, stale report that is days old?"

Prowler, sensing the growing fury of his Dragon Lord, answered with excuses. "I tried to find you, but you were back to searching to and fro across the earth. It has only been . . . " Prowler paused, then whimpered, "I'm afraid I've lost track of the weeks."

"Lost track of the weeks? *Weeks?*" Lord Dragon shouted back, the force of his hot breath engulfing the lesser dragon. Prowler cringed at the foul stench and prepared himself for another blast.

Lord Dragon took in a deep breath and let loose on Prowler. "Not hours, not days—you've lost track of weeks? He could be anywhere!"

Without a further word, the greater dragon thrust his bony wings down with all his might and shot up into the sky like a rocket, leaving Prowler shielding his face from the dust cloud below. Prowler watched him speed like lightning toward the wasteland.

*****

Nick, lost in thought, didn't realize that he had been rolling the golf ball around between his palm and the mattress until he came to a chapter break and looked down. He put the book down and brought the ball up to look at it again. Half of the ball was golden, like a brass doorknob. The other side was the standard white. Nick turned the ball and read the word "Ping" and the number "3," both printed in black letters and centered on the golden side. Nick rubbed his finger below the number and felt the familiar gash.

Bitterlous swooped down and whispered, *"He's never coming back."*

He's never coming back reverberated in Nick's head.

Tears dropped from his eyes. Nick wiped them away with his hand and sniffed to keep from needing a tissue. He looked back down at the ball. A narrow black line circled the ball, dividing the white and gold. He turned the ball until he saw the eye—a thin black outline of an eye printed on the ball—staring up at him. "It's your fault!" he shouted, half to the ball and half into the air. "I hate you."

Arrogance snickered and called out, *"He doesn't care, you know? You're nothing to him. That is why he let him die."*

"Throw it away. Toss it out the window," Bitterlous joined in. *"Be rid of him once and for all. Nobody cares. Open the window and throw it out with all your might."*

"You're all alone!" Bitterlous went in for the kill and continued, *"He took your father from you."*

"I hate you," Nick said and sprang to his feet. He flipped the lock and slid open the sash. In a moment the window screen bounced from the frame onto the ground below with a thud.

Nick looked down one last time at the ball, not noticing the split-second flash of light that lit the room like a bolt of lightning from a distant storm. Nick looked back out the window and wound up like a major league pitcher to hurl the ball as far down the hill outside as he could throw it. In that moment, a guardian shot into the room and spun the ball in his hand, so when Nick tightened his grip on the ball to throw, his thumb fell upon the familiar gash. He crumpled to the floor.

"I miss you," Nick said as he closed his eyes, forcing tears to fall. Down deep inside he wished he hadn't stolen the ball, but was too afraid to return it now. He shut his eyes, squinting against a fresh drizzle of tears, and held the ball against his chest as he wept.

*****

From the back deck Mary heard the muffled shouts of her son. She shifted in her seat, itching to check on Nick and see what he was doing in his room. Was he reading the book? Was he sulking in a corner with his earphones in? She had earlier heard him shuffling around in the kitchen and knew he had found her peace offering. But what of it? Was she just giving him an excuse to further isolate himself by letting him eat in his room?

"Maybe I should go check on him," she mused aloud. "He's been in there for at least two hours now."

"Don't go back there yet," her mother softly interjected from the seat next to her. "The boy needs time alone."

Mary paused. "I just want to see if he's okay."

"Leave him be. He's working it out. The boy probably doesn't know it yet, but he's in a wrestling match with God back there."

The wise words of experience comforted Mary. She leaned over to her mom, kissed her wrinkled forehead and smiled. "I'm sure glad I'm not alone."

Anna pointed up with her index finger. "We're never alone." Neither could see the guardian standing watch behind the elderly woman's chair.

*****

Nick's phone buzzed, but the vibration, muted by the quilted bedspread, didn't stir Nick this time. Something deep inside of him was cracking, softening, with each page he turned. The more furious the Lord Dragon became, the more Nick was taken aback with the familiar refrain of the monster's rage. He recognized it as the same poison that had been spewing from his own heart.

The phone buzzed a second time, but still Nick didn't notice. Without warning, a rush of cold air blew in from the window. A storm front was passing through, and billowing gray clouds rolled across the horizon. Strangely, Nick felt they mirrored the tempest going on inside him.

Nervous at the contemplative look Bitterlous observed on Nick's face, the shadowy figure launched a few choice seeds toward Nick in the shape of whispered phrases designed to twist and carve their way deeper into the recesses of his heart.

"It's not fair," hissed the first granule. *"You deserve a better life."*

"God must not care about you," echoed the second seed. To the watching dragon's astonishment, however, the seeds barely dented the surface of Nick's heart. Change was in the air.

Chapter 13

Temptation in the Wilderness

So, dear reader, the dragon could not kill the Prince when he was a child. Every arrow he would attempt to send toward the King's son would deflect easily, for it was not yet the Appointed Time!

But with the announcement of the Promised One by his Heavenly Father, the Prince was as vulnerable to attack as any man. For he must endure temptation like us in every way.

*****

Lord Dragon traversed the canyons of the vast wasteland in search of the carpenter. With the wilderness topography printed like a map upon his mind, he narrowed his search to those areas accessible by foot. His eyes could spot movement at great distances, much like the way an eagle spies a mouse from high up in the clouds. Within an hour of beginning his search, Lord Dragon discovered his quarry kneeling on the flat sandy top of a rugged hill, facing away. He swooped down, disappearing behind a crag of rocks, stirring but a wisp of dust with his careful landing. Then he clawed his way up to the opposite ridge and peered over the edge from behind.

The carpenter looked nothing like the glorious Prince the Lord Dragon remembered. The man kneeling in front of him looked frail and gaunt, even through his tunic. If Prowler was right, the man now kneeling before him hadn't eaten in weeks.

Lord Dragon laughed to himself, remembering how he had long ago led a great company of the King's worshipers astray in this very wilderness. *Men are weak*, he thought. *Just find their weakness.*

Lord Dragon smiled. "Are you hungry?" he called out to the carpenter. "If you are the King's Son, then turn these rocks to bread."

The sudden echo of the question breaking the silence would have scared any man to death, but it didn't startle the Prince. The Prince pushed up from the sand and stood tall. Then he turned to face the voice that confronted him. Although the carpenter's lengthy fast had drained his strength and left him gaunt, Lord Dragon recognized the unmistakably regal gaze of the Son of the King.

"Turn these rocks to bread. You must be hungry. That is, if you have the strength," he hissed and taunted.

The Prince replied evenly, "It is written that man should not live by bread alone but by every word that is given by the King."

"So you are the King's Son—or were the King's Son. I see a lowly carpenter," the dragon said, but no answer came. The dragon continued his taunting.

"Have you not seen? Your people follow me and my ways. They have forgotten you." As he spoke, dragon seed poured from his mouth, covering the Prince, but not a single seed took hold. The Prince was silent.

The Lord Dragon mustered all his inner strength to manifest himself before the carpenter. Without a sound his full image appeared, deformed and grotesque, standing confident and proud upon the sand. Inside his dragon heart, his anger burned. Then without warning of any sound, he ran at the Prince, thrusting his wings backward to speed his assault. He closed the distance between them in seconds and forced the Prince over the edge of the precipice, launching them both into the air. The dragon seized him with his scaly arms. Cherubs from heaven raced to rescue the King's Son, but the Prince waved them off with one glance.

Lord Dragon saw it as a game of strategy and knew he must play within the rules. Should he drop his quarry, the guardians would easily bear him up. So placing his full trust in the power of the evil seed to corrupt a man, he carried the Prince out of the wasteland into the Temple City where he set him down upon the pinnacle of the temple.

"If you are the King's Son, throw yourself down from here," his black speech continued." For it is written that the guards of the mountain will bear you up." Lord Dragon again enticed the Prince, hoping that the seed he planted would sprout.

The Prince calmly retorted, "It is written that you shall not put your Lord to the test." The seed of the dragon found no fertile soil upon the Prince's humble heart.

Lord Dragon, seething with anger, grabbed the Prince by the shoulders and carried him off away from the city. Again he set him down, this time upon a tall mountain peak. Looking out from this vantage point, the two could see the whole of the land—from the sea on the right to the wilderness on the left with all the kingdoms in the valleys below, which lead off to the Temple City. Then Lord Dragon mustered all his pride for his greatest boast.

Lord Dragon knew that men angered easily when someone made claim of their property. In centuries past he had incited more than a hundred wars and battles by tempting men against one another, fighting over lands. Now he would use the same temptations on the Prince. Lord Dragon pointed his right hand to the far left, then panned it across the valleys as he spoke, spewing dragon seed in massive quantity.

"All these I will give to you . . . *if* you fall down and worship me," he offered. But Lord Dragon made a critical mistake. The kingdoms of the lowlands were not his to give; they were for the

Prince to rescue. Though he thought it was his strongest temptation, this, in fact, was his weakest. Not a single dragon seed came close to sprouting. Having been created by the King, the lowlands belonged to the King. Lord Dragon owned their corruption, nothing more. In time evil would be destroyed, the kingdom restored, and the dragon imprisoned within the abyss.

In a demonstration of his power over the fallen guardian, having withstood his lies, the Prince turned to the dragon and with commanding authority spoke, "Be gone!"

At once, Lord Dragon was cast down from the mountain. As he dropped to the valley below, he heard the Prince call out, "For it is written you shall worship the King, and only him will you serve."

Lord Dragon fell, now for the third time, humiliated and more furious than ever. Up above, the cherubim raced toward the Prince to celebrate his victory over the dragon and his seed.

*****

"Nick, are you OK?" came a voice from outside the door an hour later, startling the boy and causing him to jump.

"I'm . . . I'm . . . fine, Mom," Nick glanced over his shoulder but returned his gaze to the page in front of him.

"I saw you took some of the mac and cheese, but are you still hungry? I was trying to figure out when to have dinner."

Bitterlous and Arrogance circled above, patiently waiting for an opportunity to restart the conflict between the boy and his mother, but none came.

"The mac and cheese was great, Mom," Nick surprised his mom with his almost-thank-you. "I'll probably be good for awhile." Truth was, he didn't want to stop reading. Flipping the page to glance ahead, he saw the next chapter was about the man of the tombs, who was, according to the legend, his great far-off grandfather.

Outside the room Mary smiled. *He's hooked!* she thought. Then she spoke through the closed door again, "I was thinking of ordering pizza, so you just let me know when you're hungry again."

Nick sat stunned. Pizza and mac and cheese in the same day? Wasn't he grounded for weeks? What was getting into his mom? Well, he wouldn't turn this down. "Sounds good. Anytime will do. I could eat a few slices." Then he added, "Thanks, Mom."

"Thanks, Mom?" Mary whispered her son's words aloud in disbelief. *I should have given him that book months ago.*

Chapter 14

The Man of the Tombs

Here, reader, is where we get to the heart of our family story. Where I, Tymar, will take you on Demas's journey. The King has given us this story so we can see and understand. The human heart has not changed from ancient times. The dragon seeds still take root and fill us with anger, pride, and selfishness. If you do not carefully apply the Antidote, fellow traveler, his story will become yours. The dragon delights in taking out as many of us as he can, thwarting our usefulness to the King and stealing the praise that belongs to his majesty.

*****

Young Demas walked down the familiar road to his home under cover of the pitch-black evening, drawn to the lamplight pouring forth from the front window opening. He touched his palms to the rough wooden planks and pressed his whole weight evenly up against the door. Slowly pushing it, a little at a time, he hoped the heavy iron hinges wouldn't squeak. The door opened without a sound. Demas relaxed.

At that same moment, a guardian of the King, who up to this time had watched over the boy, conceded defeat. It had been another rough evening. Dragon roots filled the young lad's heart.

Only the King himself could save the lost boy now. As soon as the guardian departed, the dragon, who also watched the lad, flew in for the kill.

"Demas, is that you?" The voice of his mother startled Demas. The fact she waited up for him annoyed the boy.

Why can't she just leave me alone? he thought. "What do you want?"

"It's past midnight. I've been sitting here worried that robbers got hold of you," she said, blocking his way just inside the door.

"I didn't tell you to stay up. Just go to bed next time."

Demas pushed her aside to get through. He didn't want to listen to what she had to say. Neither of them perceived the evil shadow that slipped through the open door and circled the young man.

Arrogance, one of the most cunning dragons in Legion's command, whispered to Demas, spewing dragon seed upon his heart. *"There she goes trying to control your life. You're not a child anymore. You can take care of yourself."* The seed sprouted as soon as it hit his pride-riddled heart. The fresh shoots of the sprouting dragon seed slithered across the tangle of older roots, searching for any opening to his heart. Then, finding small openings, they plunged down to burrow in what little space was left.

"I'm not a child anymore, Mom," Demas said. "You don't have to be waiting up for me. I can take care of myself." Arrogance smiled, knowing the fresh seed had taken hold yet again by the nature of the boy's sharp disrespect.

Emmaliah grasped her son's arm, just below the shoulder. "I told you that if you didn't come home on time, you would not be permitted to leave the house after the evening meal. We'll enforce that tomorrow. You're required to remain within these walls."

The new roots plunged deeper entwining with the tangle already consuming his heart. *It would be impossible to pull them out now,* Arrogance reasoned as he shot around Demas. Demas turned away from his mother, breaking her hold. Arrogance whispered another temptation, *"You can leave, you know. She can't stop you. Why stay here and . . . "*

Before the dragon could finish, Demas shouted back, "You can't tell me what to do! I'm not a baby anymore. I can leave if I want. Don't try to stop me."

*****

A chill ran down Nick's spine. *Those were the same words I spoke,* he remembered. He reviewed the conversation from earlier in the morning. *I said the same things to my mom.* In that moment a terrible realization came to him. *I heard the same voice.*

A pang of fear shot through Nick, chilling him to his very core. He scanned the room, looking for shadows and saw none. Bitterlous and Arrogance swirled above. Then without warning Nick spun around from his bed and whispered forcefully into the air, "I will not listen to the dragon's lies." The shadowy figures suddenly fled the room like a puff of smoke. The first inklings of peace began to settle upon Nick's soul, and the fear started to gradually drain away.

How long have I been listening to lies? How long have I been obeying the voice of evil? Nick could sense a war within his soul. He wanted to say no to the temptations, but wasn't yet ready to give up his right to live and control his own life.

*****

"When your father returns from the sea tomorrow morning he will hear about this." Emmaliah would not back down in the face of her son's defiance.

"That's all he ever does, come home to yell at me," Demas sneered back.

As their voices rose and tempers kindled, the all-too-familiar argument woke Demas's older brother, Noah, who jumped out of bed to defend his mother. He was beyond exasperated at the boy's disrespect. "Why is it every time you walk into this house you start an argument?"

"Stay out of this, Noah," the younger brother snapped. "You're not in charge of me."

Emmaliah stepped between them. "That's enough, both of you. Demas, your father works hard to support us. You have no right to be disrespectful."

Demas shot her a smoldering look, arms crossed, but didn't comment.

"Listen," Emmaliah paused, softening her tone as she touched Demas on the shoulder. "We are all part of this family. One of us can't just throw off the rest of us in such disregard."

Demas pulled away. "Just leave me alone."

"You're an arrogant boy," Noah said, shaking his head in disbelief that his brother would be so selfish. Arrogance swirled above, delighted by the entire exchange.

"You better watch what you say. You'll be sorry," Demas pointed his finger at his older brother with contempt.

"Demas. Please don't speak to your older brother that way. He's not some street kid friend of yours."

Arrogance swooped in and whispered. *You don't have to put up with this. She is disrespecting your friends now.*

"I've had enough of this. I'm out of here!" Demas spat out. "You can't speak about my friends that way." The furious boy thrust open the door and ran into the black night. The dragon followed. It was not first time he had walked out the door in such a rage.

Tears began to silently run down Emmaliah's face as she stood staring at the empty doorway. She knew it was useless to go after her son when his anger boiled over.

Noah put his arm around his mom. "It's not right that he is so disrespectful," he said. *I'm sure glad that I'm not so foolish*, he thought.

"I just hope he's safe," Emmaliah said, then strained to see the last of his tan-colored tunic fade into the darkness. With her attention focused out the door, she didn't notice the shadow enter above her and circle wildly about her older son.

After a few days Demas returned, but it wasn't long until he was gone again. Demas spent little time with his family over the next several months. The bitterness he felt towards his parents grew. The time he spent together with his brother and their neighborhood friends all but ended, while the amount of time Demas spent with a new group of friends increased. It was just the same to his older brother who grew to despise his younger sibling's rebellion and his new set of friends.

Both his mother and father pleaded with Demas again and again to return, but he always balked at their rules. He began to drink, not much at first, always believing Arrogance's lies that he could stop anytime he wanted. In time, his explosive anger terrorized even his friends. They could sense the presence of the dragon possessing his heart. Demas drank every day, all day, and what little control he had was gone.

Arrogance continued tempting Demas, leading him further and further into darkness until finally Demas was fully under his control. The dragon took up full residence in the boy's heart and invited his shadowy friends to help him wreak complete havoc over the lad. A growing number of dragons tormented Demas for sport, ever spewing fresh dragon seed upon his heart. They drove him into mad rages.

Demas challenged anyone who stood against him and often got into fights with the other town riffraff. During such altercations, the dragons sent him into wild rages. He pounded much larger and stronger men with no regard for pain nor care for his bones, which he broke often. Several times the local garrison arrested him and locked him up in chains and irons, but Demas broke the chains and escaped into the hills that bordered the sea. In the end, he lived in the empty tombs cut into the rock of the hills, robbing those who wandered near him.

Legion wrestled control of Demas from Arrogance and welcomed the dragons he commanded in. The young man became a party home for his dragon forces during their boasting celebrations where their evil shadows passed in and out of his root-infested heart at will. A hundred or more could possess him at one time. The dragon forces took turns throwing Demas into crazed convulsions, while others hovered over him howling in delight. There among the tombs they could revel all night, certain to be left alone, for no one traveled there.

Demas, who lived in constant torment, forgot all memory of home. The dragons never let up except for the short breaks where they slept off their intoxication or toyed with a second man whom Arrogance also led astray. That allowed their captives to rest in turn. In those moments of peace, Demas experienced relief. Although exhausted, he fought off sleeping long enough to wander away from the tombs down to the seashore below. The sound of the water lapping on the shore soothed his troubled mind and allowed him some brief rest. Demas never got far or slept long before the dragons returned to torment him again.

While sightings of Demas walking among the tombs were uncommon, it happened often enough that local parents began to warn their children not to talk back in disrespect and arrogance, lest they too suffer the same fate as the *man of the tombs*.

Demas had one wish. He wished he'd never allowed the dragon seed to grow in the first place. But as the years passed, his mind and memory deteriorated and visits to the seashore grew less frequent. The dragon roots all but consumed his heart and mind, choking any spark of hope.

He was lost . . . until the day the Son of the King landed a fishing boat on the shore, not far from the caves where he lived.

*****

Legion called a gathering of all his dragon forces. Prior to their reporting session, the dragons played their sport with Demas and the other man in turns, sending them both into rages again and again over several hours without a break. When the two of them collapsed, Legion called the horde to attention and addressed the company of dragons in his command.

"The carpenter is indeed the Son of the King of the Mountain. Of this, we can be certain. Dragon seed has no effect upon him and his increasing power is reversing the curse. Wherever he goes, he heals people. The lame walk, the blind see, the deaf hear and . . . " Legion paused, looked around, and thought for a moment about the two men lying exhausted in the midst of the horde. Convinced both men, tormented for years were all but dragons now, he finished his thought, "The carpenter is casting our fellow dragons out of the people we possess."

Demas heard the report but did not dare open his eyes.

The dragon horde shrunk back in disbelief, though rumors circulated of such failures among their rank. Deceptor stepped forward to offer supporting testimony.

"I possessed a young man and drove him into a gathering at the temple to spread fear among the faithful. When the carpenter entered, he cast me out with but a few words. He broke my hold and dissolved the dragon roots within the young man that took me months to cultivate and grow. The carpenter might look like an ordinary man, but he wields the authority of the King. He is the Prince we all despise. With my last grip upon my host I shouted out his identity, 'I know that you are the Holy Son of the King!' I cried. Do not be fooled. The Prince, while living in the lowlands retains the authority to cast us into the Abyss."

The dragon horde grew silent at the report. Then Deceptor shouted in fear, "He is too powerful for us. Too powerful for us, I tell you. Flee and scatter, he is going to send us back to the . . . "

"Silence!" Legion commanded. "Get him out of here. We don't have time for weakness."

Two stronger dragons grabbed Deceptor and carried him away from the assembly, but his warning spread fear in the hearts of the weaker-minded dragons.

Legion knew he must rally his forces. "We will destroy the Prince, I tell you," Legion said, regaining his command of their attention.

"How can we destroy him if his power is greater than ours?" a lesser dragon inquired.

"Silence!" Legion rebuked the subordinate, then lifted his voice for all to hear. "For the moment, the power of the carpenter is greater than ours, that much is true. He has thwarted our plans and frustrated our rebellion. He uses humility to keep our dragon seed from sprouting. But Lord Dragon's been watching him and has discovered a weakness. That is why I called you together tonight."

The word *weakness* drew their attention. The dragons listened carefully for Legion's explanation.

Legion continued. "The carpenter may not fear us, but he is afraid of his fellow men. In order to fulfill the prophecy and strike against the Dragon Lord's heel, he had to be born in human flesh. He can still command us dragons and has actively opposed us, but he is powerless against the strength of man. Do you remember when they tried to throw him over the cliff? The Prince did not call down fire upon them nor did he issue a command, but he slipped away and hid."

The dragons began to talk among themselves. It was true. Not a single dragon ever saw or heard the Prince strike against another man, but he did cast out many a dragon.

Legion could see excitement growing for battle within the horde as he finished the report. "He tires at the end of the day. He thirsts and becomes hungry. His flesh bleeds like that of all men. He will die!"

Arrogance, who didn't follow the commander's logic, questioned, "If it is true that he has power over us, how will we kill him?"

"We will not kill him," Legion answered. "The people he created will. They will destroy him."

With this revelation the horde erupted with all sorts of screaming jeers. Man killing man. The idea delighted them to no end.

Legion continued his address, "The dragon seed first cast by Lord Dragon is spreading throughout the land. No one can stop it. As I speak, the religious rulers are plotting to take the carpenter's life. One of the men from the carpenter's inner circle is stealing from their common purse. Though he appears as loyal as the others, his heart is twisted with dragon seed roots. Lord Dragon will possess him when the time is right. The Prince will be betrayed by one of his own. Then we will have our revenge against the King."

"The religious rulers are under our control. On the outside, they appear as holy men, dedicated to the King, but inside dragon roots are turning all their hearts to stone. We've got them plotting his death. They only lack the nerve to do it themselves. But their anger and jealousy are growing stronger by the day. Soon, the carpenter will die."

The demon horde howled. Lord Dragon was a genius. They would use the carpenter's own people against him. Once he was dead, the light atop the mountain would grow dark, and the dragons would rule over all. The dragons flew into a frenzy, intoxicated with their revenge.

While they celebrated, their hold over Demas relaxed. *I must find the carpenter. He can set me free.* He felt a flicker of hope. The dragons coursing like a cloud of bats in the sky above paid Demas no mind. But the other man, always wary of Demas, kept his eye upon him.

The dragons reveled late into the night discussing various means by which the religious rulers might destroy the Prince. Some favored stoning while others enjoyed the idea of throwing the carpenter off a cliff. But once Legion mentioned the idea of impaling him upon a tree, army style, the dragons flew into a frenzy. Intoxicated with their celebration, they grew tired and fell asleep.

Demas had already begun his escape. He crawled away from the graves toward the sea, moving ever so slowly, fearing to wake the dragons within and without. Demas sped up in order to reach the taller grass, now only twenty feet ahead. He hoped the thick cover would hide him.

Just before his last foot passed out of sight, the second man opened his eyes and caught sight of Demas. Sanctimonious, the dragon who for long years possessed the second man was also awake and aware. The seasoned dragon thought about shouting to alert the others of the escape, but seeking Legion's commendation, he set off to capture Demas single-handed. Once he held him in his grasp, he would sound the alarm.

Chapter 15

Into the Swine

Mary walked back into the room, wiping her eyes. "Well, Mom, I think he's reading the story. He even said thank you for the pizza." Her eyes met her mother's comforting gaze. "We're at a crossroads, and I don't know what to do. I'm so afraid of making the wrong move. I've been walking around praying. Praying like crazy."

"Me too, honey," Anna nodded, lifting a shaky hand to steady her glasses. "I haven't stopped praying all day. Nick is either going to let God be in charge of his life or he's going to keep trying to take charge himself. Not so different from what that dragon did so long ago. Now if you don't mind, I'll take a slice of that pizza; the mac and cheese is freezing by now."

"Oh, Mom, I'm so sorry! I've been thinking about Nick all day and forgot that we need to eat too. Let me get us a couple of plates, and I'll bring it in."

*****

Once Demas traveled deep into the taller grass, he paused to rest. The spongy soil at the base of the plants soothed the abrasions he received crawling over the rocky ground during his escape. He pressed on, crawling from tomb to tomb, until he passed the last of the caves cut into the rock of the mountain that bordered the sea. The further he fled from the dragons, the better he felt.

After what seemed like an hour of crawling over patches of jagged rock shards, the cool sand soothed his aching hands. He paused to rest again. *Soon I'll reach the hill that leads down to the water's edge*, he thought and purposed to press on. He was eager to hear the sound of the waves breaking on the shore.

As he pulled himself forward, a voice called from behind.

"Where do you think you're going?"

Demas didn't answer. He mustered his strength and crawled faster to escape.

"You cannot get away. You'll run into the sea. Then I'll drag you back to the tombs."

Demas recognized the voice of Sanctimonious, now just behind him, speaking through the other man he had possessed. He had to get away.

"Leave me alone!" Demas shouted back as he kicked against his attacker, striking his outstretched hand.

Back at the tombs, a sudden strong beam of light snapped Legion out of his rest. His head spun from side to side, and he noticed for the first time that the two men were gone.

Legion alerted his forces, then thrust down his wings and flew off. One by one, the other dragons sprang to their feet. In turn they passed the message, "The prisoners have escaped!" Wisps of shadow rose across the field in search of the two men. From his vantage point high above the commotion, Legion caught sight of the two men wrestling on the bluff, overlooking the sandy shore.

Within minutes, Legion thrust his shadow upon Demas and commanded him to return to the tombs. Demas fought against Legion and refused him. But Legion's power sent Demas convulsing to the ground. Still the young man resisted the dragon's commands to turn back to the tombs. He stretched out his hands, grasping for tussocks of grass to pull himself up and over the edge. The second man, thrown off by the convulsions, took hold of Demas by the shoulder to pull him back away from the ledge. Demas wrestled against him upon the crest of the hill, while he also battled against Legion in his mind.

The other dragons, drawn to the altercation, sped down and forced their shadows upon Demas. The dragons joined the fight for control of Demas, but it was too late. The carpenter and his boatful of friends had just stepped onto the sand. The grip of the dragons upon the souls of the men began to weaken; the men gained strength. Now both of the men battled against their oppressors.

With his last measure of strength, Demas pulled himself over the edge and tumbled down the bank to the shore. The other man fell with him, grasping his foot.

As he rolled, Demas caught a glimpse of the carpenter. The small spark of hope he held deep inside burst into flame. He believed that the carpenter could deliver him. Demas fought and fought against the dragons' commands while he stumbled his way toward the sea.

The dragon horde did not give in. They renewed the fight and threw themselves into a frenzy, overpowering their host and sending Demas into a mad rage. The tormented man screamed and fell to the ground, writhing in pain. Farther away from the sea the other possessed man also jerked and twisted in agony.

The carpenter stepped toward Demas. His friends from the boat stood behind him, waiting to see what he would do. Several fishermen and two pig farmers, who had come into the village to sell their swine wandered over and were joined by a growing crowd of villagers. The sharp-pitched screams of the two tormented men were difficult to ignore.

"Come out of them," the carpenter said, commanding the dragons.

Demas twisted in the sand as Legion cried through his voice, "What have you to do with me, Son of the Most High?"

"What is your name?" the carpenter demanded.

"My name is Legion, for we are many."

Demas could feel the dragons within gripping and clawing to keep their hold. He looked up into the carpenter's eyes, ashamed of who he had become. But strangely, a sensation of love filled his root-infested, rocky heart. He barely recognized it. It seemed like years since he had felt love.

Losing their grip upon Demas, the dragons became crazed within him, forcing his body once again to convulse on the ground. Several of them spoke. "Do not send us into the abyss," they shouted. "Send us to the swine; let us enter them."

With nervous foreboding, the farmers instinctively turned to check on their pigs, which appeared well under the control of the swine herders back on top the steep bank. Still they were concerned something terrible would come of the evil display.

Hoping to reach the carpenter, the second possessed man mustered his strength. He rose from the ground and extended his open hand toward him, then collapsed of exhaustion.

The carpenter pointed to the pigs and shouted, "Go." At once the dragons writhed out of their hosts with a deafening shriek. Both men lay motionless on the ground, as still as the dead.

Further back by the boat, the fishermen gasped but kept their distance. The farmers ran to their swine, which began squealing and running about, savagely breaking free of the herders' control.

Branch by branch the dragon roots within the two men shriveled and dissolved to nothing. Their hearts filled with joy as their reason returned. Now they knew beyond doubt that the carpenter who had set them free was indeed the Prince, the Son of the King.

For the first time in many years, Demas smiled. A pungent odor of fish and warm sand delighted him. The dragons, by this time swirling and raging through the pigs, drove the animals mad down the steep bank, away from the herders, crashing them into the sea where they drowned.

Demas pushed himself up from the ground and glanced down at his hands, amazed. They were soft, free of wounds, and bore no scars. He turned toward the Prince, who stepped forward with open arms. Demas threw himself upon the soft cotton tunic. As he did, the Prince wrapped his arms around his ragged clothes. While his clothing remained tattered, the foul odor that clung to his body was gone, washed clean. Demas was free.

"Let me return with you," Demas asked.

"You cannot come with us," the Prince replied. "I have work for you to do here."

"I beg you. I have nothing here."

"Oh, but you do," the Prince warmly smiled at the man. "Go home to your friends and family and tell them how much the Prince has done for you, and how he has had mercy on you." Then the Prince touched his head and called him the name he had not heard since he was a small child, "Be at peace, Nicodemus."

*****

Nick threw his head back into the headboard and dropped the book. "Nicodemus," he said. "That's my name!" He looked at the ceiling and thought some more.

"Is it true?" The same question that Mary had asked her mother escaped his lips.

Is he my grandfather? I mean my far-off, long-ago grandfather? Nick pondered the implications of the deeper question. *Does the Prince love me this much too? Can he bring me back from what I've become?*

Just then, he heard a knock at the door.

"It's me," Mary said.

Nick jumped up and opened the door.

Mary delivered him a plate with two large meat lover's pizza slices—his absolute favorite. The smell of molten cheese, sausage, pepperoni, and oregano filled the bedroom as Mary passed a plate with two large slices to her son.

Before she could turn to leave, Nick questioned his mom. "Is it true?"

"The story? Of course, it's true," Mary replied.

"Not the story. Is he my grandfather? My far-off, long-ago grandfather?"

"Look," she said. "I'll tell you what Mom-Mom told me, 'What does it matter? He was somebody's grandfather, living among the tombs, possessed by evil, hearing voices all the day long until he was set free.'"

"All I know," Mary continued, "is that my father passed the story to me, saying his father passed it to him, and now I have passed it to you. Nick, I believe the story. I believe it's true because I sense shadows lurking all around us."

Mary drew close to her son and hugged him, careful not to knock the pizza from his hand. She smiled as she pulled away, noticing that Nick was hugging her back with his free hand. As she turned to walk back out into the hall, a chill ran down her spine as she caught a quick glimpse of the lump in her son's shirt pocket. *The ball*, she thought as she continued turning to leave. *It must be the ball.* She dared not look back around. She pulled the door closed and walked away.

Nick looked down at the pizza. He had the best mom in the world. *Why on earth do I get so angry?* he wondered. Minutes later the pizza was gone, and he was back to the story. He turned the page, eager to continue reading.

*****

Demas, amazed that the Prince knew his full name, pulled back from the embrace and looked up into his eyes. "Friends? Family?" Demas asked out loud, confused. "They want nothing to do with me."

"Don't be so sure, Demas. They've never stopped loving you. Go home and tell them how much has been done for you. The both of you."

The both of you? Demas repeated the Prince's words, completely confused until the second man called his name.

"Demas," the second man said as he rose from the sand.

Demas snapped his head around; he knew that voice.

"Demas, it's me."

"Noah?" Demas stood stunned. *How? Why?* He thought, then took off running toward his older brother.

Chapter 16

The Rescue

Lord Dragon stood tall, encouraging his forces, who were gathered on the flat with open tombs cut into the hill behind them. His body, scarred from burning, smelled of sulfur. Even his voice, damaged by the heat of the abyss, sounded as if gravel turned inside his throat with every word.

"His own people will kill him," he said.

The dragons chanted, "Kill him! Kill him! Kill him!" Then dragon roots erupted from of each of their hearts, burst through their scales and coursed their way down to the ground like living vines spreading everywhere. The advancing roots fingered their way across the countryside searching for someone to devour. The main trunks grew larger and sent out more wicked roots. It was as though ten years of ivy growth spread across the field in a moment. The black roots spread for one purpose—to kill. As they coursed their way across the land, thin tendrils searched every home, stable, and building for any opening.

One house, made of stone with a solid wood door and shutters on the windows, was closed up and seemed impenetrable. The vine-like roots grew around it searching the threshold for any crack, but the craftsman who constructed the house built it well. The roots covered the stone and windows and, finding no entry, coursed up and onto the roof to a single entry point—an open chimney. With no fire to repel their advance, the black roots shot down the flue and filled the home, then burst open the window shutters and door and continued to spread, searching for their ultimate prize—the Prince.

"The Prince! They are going to kill him!" Demas shouted as he shot up in his bed from a deep sleep, his heart pounding from the nightmare. He ran his fingers through his hair as he realized he had been dreaming. He looked about the room. A warm glow from the oil lamp he left burning cast enough light for him to see that all was well. The nightmare jarred his memory, bringing forward scenes from his past. He moved to the table to jot down a few clues. Day by day Demas remembered more and more of his ordeal as a captive of the dragons.

He spoke aloud the words he suddenly remembered. "One of his inner circle is stealing from their common purse, his heart twisted with dragon seed roots," he reflected and struggled to know what to do. Now more than ever, Demas was convinced the dragons were plotting to kill the promised Son of the King.

I have to warn him, Demas thought. His mind raced in all directions as he tried to come up with a plan. It had been nine months since he and his brother were set free from the dragons.

A simple plan came together in his mind as Demas packed a few things for his journey. The annual feast was but a few days away, so transportation to the Temple City would be easy to find. Everyone with a cart would offer themselves to pilgrims. He would hire a wagon to take him there. Along the way, he could welcome travelers to join him. Thankful for the free ride, the travelers would be glad to talk. Perhaps someone might know where he could find the carpenter whose popularity ever grew among the common folk.

Within the hour, Demas hired a mule cart and driver and set off traveling west toward the mountains. Once up and through the higher pass, the way south to the Temple City took one additional day. If all went well, Demas reasoned, he would reach the city by Thursday morning. He tossed his cloak into the back of the cart and gave the driver the required fare.

"If you see a weary traveler or two struggling up the hill or walking all alone, welcome them into the wagon," Demas said. "I'll cover any additional fee. I'm eager to hear fresh news from the Temple City.

The driver nodded. As he climbed into the cart, Demas addressed the driver and qualified his instruction. "Only no wandering vagrants. I'm interested in honorable conversation," Demas said. He looked for the cleanest spot in the back of the wagon and sat down. The old wood smelled of hay and animals, perhaps that is why it was so easy to acquire. Still, Demas was glad to be on his way. The driver slapped the reins against the mule and the cart lunged forward.

"What brings you to the city?" Thaddeus, the mule driver, asked over his shoulder. Demas sat in the cart trying to keep his balance as the cart lurched back and forth, starting its climb up the hill toward the pass. He grabbed the rough side of the cart with his right hand before turning to speak to the driver.

"I'm looking to meet up with a friend who grew up as a carpenter on this side of the sea," Demas said, raising his voice over the rumble of the wheels on the loose stone.

"Most of the folks traveling this way will be headed for the Temple City for the feast to worship at the Temple. That is where you'll find the carpenter."

"You know him?"

"I haven't met the man, but folks in the city can't stop talking about him. They say he is the one who will break a curse and lead the King's people to victory in battle. Some believe he is the Prince from the King who lives high atop the mountain." The driver pointed off in the distance at the base of the cliffs that shot up and disappeared into the clouds.

"The latest news, though I find it hard to believe, is that he commanded a dead man to rise from a grave—and the guy walked straight out of the tomb! Everyone is talking about it. Some say there were a hundred witnesses, and the man had been dead for at least three days. If that is true, then perhaps he is the Prince, but the stories you hear on the road are not so reliable."

"He is the Prince, I tell you. I know it, for he delivered me."

Demas shared his whole story with Thaddeus, who listened obligingly. The driver thanked Demas for sharing, then for some time the two of them kept silent, giving the conversation a rest. As the cart thumped along the road, Demas reflected, as he often did, on the years he lost. He thought about the deceptive nature of pride. His own rebellion and fall were easier to understand. But what often puzzled him more was his brother's downfall. Everyone could see the bad fruit of rebellious disrespect, but the self-righteous roots that twisted in his brother's heart grew undetected for years.

Demas remembered how folks doted over his brother saying, "You're such a good little boy." Little did they realize they were feeding a growing arrogance and self-righteousness.

Growing up, it seemed that Noah never did anything wrong. He was a model student, helped around the house, and never spoke a word of disrespect. But inside his heart the dragons spread their seed to sprout just the same. And worse, the roots grew completely undetected. The result was that Noah believed himself to be better than others. Into that heart one of the most cunning dragons of all, Sanctimonious, breathed his lies, sowing the seeds of self-confidence and self-glory.

Noah excelled at everything and secured a good job as a foreman of a large farming operation. He ran the farm with a heartless strictness and fired anyone who broke the rules. He became rich with money but was bankrupt of good friends. In the end, no one could stand Noah's constant judging of others. His wife abandoned him, leaving Noah the laughingstock of the community. They called him a hypocrite, which opened the door for the dragons to spread the seeds of self-pity and self-destruction, which ultimately drove him to the tombs.

Remembering the darkness of those days made Demas grateful for the Prince. After their deliverance, Noah's family and friends welcomed him home. Who would have believed that in a few months' time, Noah would reconcile with his wife? The power of grace and forgiveness were amazing.

Demas turned his thoughts to his own life. He awoke with joy every morning and loved to breathe in the fresh air. But he was lonely and wished for a wife he could share his life with. He envied his brother and wondered if he would ever have a son to pass along the truth he'd learned and the story of how the Prince had rescued him.

Though he didn't show it, Thaddeus too reflected on the story Demas shared as he drove the mules. He didn't put much stock in what he called traveler's gossip. But by the end of the story Thaddeus found the tale hard to dismiss. He didn't mention it to Demas, but he had heard the story of the man of the tombs and the stampede of swine down the hillside from a number of Gadarans. The whole tale stirred a desire within to meet the carpenter Prince for himself.

The two men didn't discuss the story again, though they did converse briefly about this or that. Demas rode alone in the back of the cart that first day without a single traveler signaling to them for a ride. Demas inquired as to why the driver could not secure a second passenger.

"The pilgrims," he explained, "want no part of the market cart. For it's well known that I carry swine in the fall to market. They believe pigs are dirty and repulsive. It will be much easier for us to pick up a second passenger or two tomorrow, when we reach Sychar."

"They call Sychar the city of outcasts," the driver said over his shoulder, offering a bit of trivia. "Folks there will be glad for a ride," he said.

As it got closer to evening, Demas passed the time watching the other travelers they passed by. Those under the dragon's influence were usually easy to spot, even without them saying a word. They often scowled at each other and rarely smiled. Demas could discern the evil hanging about them. He tried not to look into their eyes for fear that one of the dragons might recognize him.

They stopped for the night under a grove of olive trees. Demas fell asleep in the bed of the cart, the driver under a tree. Their second day also ended without picking up a single traveler. But soon into the third day, on the other side of the city of outcasts, Thaddeus called the mules to a stop and pulled off to the side. "Need a ride?" he asked a group of three women traveling alone.

One of the women scanned the cart. She could see the mules were well cared for. Only then did he speak. "What is your fare?" she inquired, hoisting her sack a little higher on her shoulder. She was clearly the leader of the group.

Demas, whom the women hadn't noticed because he was reclining in the cart, turned, looked over the side, and answered, "Free to weary travelers headed to the Temple City."

His sudden address startled the travelers, who took a step back. The woman who had spoken looked warily at Demas and could tell that he was not a pilgrim.

"Who are you?" she questioned intently.

"My name is Demas. Are you ladies traveling to the Temple City for the feast?"

Demas's willingness to offer his name and his pleasant tone slightly disarmed the woman. "Yes," she finally conceded.

"May I ask your name?" Demas asked.

"I am Shoshanna. And these are a few friends from my village." She gave her name against her better judgment, but Demas seemed to be an honest man. "You are not a pilgrim," she asserted, still unsure about accepting a ride. "What business does a man from Gadara have in the Temple City, traveling with an empty cart?"

"You are observant," Demas said. "I'm hoping to find a man many call the carpenter, a man who has healed the sick and set many free. I believe he is the Prince come to destroy the curse and restore the land."

Of course! I should have recognized the work of the Prince in this man, Shoshanna thought.

"I spoke to him about a year ago. Or should I say, he spoke to me," Shoshanna offered. "That is why my friends and I are traveling to the Temple City. We would like to meet him again."

"Then we shall travel together." Demas reached down and offered Shoshanna his hand.

"I can manage," she said. Shoshanna ignored his extended hand and climbed up into the wagon herself. Her two friends reluctantly joined her, but didn't offer their names.

*****

The smell of fresh tomato sauce filled the house below. Traditional Italian music played in the background. Martha knew she wouldn't be leaving anytime soon. Nobody escaped dinner at the Rossi house if Mia's mom had any say in the matter.

Mrs. Rossi smiled as Martha entered the kitchen followed closely by her daughter.

"You're not leaving us? I just finished a homemade lasagna and put it in the oven. It will be done in a half-hour or forty minutes." As she spoke, she walked up to Martha, took the backpack off her shoulders, and continued, "I'll call your mother and ask if you can stay." She pulled her phone out of her striped kitchen apron and started to search for Mary's number.

"Did you buy a new phone, Mrs. Rossi?" Martha asked noticing a tab of plastic film, which covered the screen, dangling off the end.

"No, they gave it to me for free. All I had to do was extend my contract."

"What did you do with your old phone?" Martha asked. Mia shot her a glance from behind her mother's back as she waved her palm across her neck, giving Martha the signal to cut the comments.

"I tucked it away in a drawer. Just in case this new one breaks before the contract expires," she replied, then pushed a few buttons on the phone and held it up to her face.

"Hello, Mary? This is Rosa Rossi," Mrs. Rossi shouted into the phone. With the phone's volume set at its highest level the girls could hear Martha's mom reply.

"Hi, Rosa. Is everything alright? I completely forgot about Martha—and it's past dinnertime."

"Everything is fine. I was calling about dinner. Martha would like to stay here and join us. The girls have been studying all afternoon."

"Oh, wonderful," Mary replied.

"I made a fresh lasagna. Marco and the boys are out tonight, so we've got plenty to spare."

"Of course, she can stay. I'm so grateful Martha has such good friends to hang out with. We ordered out for pizza, so Martha won't miss much."

"Pizza? Why don't you all come over for dinner, there is plenty for everyone."

"Oh, that is so kind of you, but Mom is not as mobile as she used to be. But I would love it if you would send a bit home with Martha. I love real Italian food and yours is the best."

Martha smiled. Her mom knew just how to decline an offer with grace.

"I will send home enough for you, your mom, and Nick too."

"Thank you so much. Tell Martha I said hi and not to stay too late."

"Don't worry, we'll send her off after dinner. God bless," Mrs. Rossi said, closing the phone and dropping it into her apron pocket. "Your mother sends her love, Martha."

"Thank you so much for inviting me to stay for dinner. Your food is amazing," Martha said and smiled politely.

Mia rolled her eyes but was glad the subject of the conversation turned away from the phone.

"Go over to the sink, you two, and wash up. I've got a platter of antipasto in the fridge."

Martha walked over to the large double sink. Mia followed. The right side was stacked with dishes piled high with a colander balancing on top of the heap. She turned on the water and washed her hands. Mia pushed in and thrust her hands under the water.

"Give me a break, Martha," Mia whispered. "If Mom finds out about the phone, I'll be stuck in this house for the next ten years."

"All you have to do is agree to stop using it to contact my brother. Do you promise?"

"I said I promise. So cut the comments."

"Good then, I won't say another word about THE PHONE," she said in a raised voice, then returned to a whisper. "Your secret is safe with me."

Mrs. Rossi set a platter of finely cut and beautifully organized Italian meats and cheeses on the table and called to the girls, "Take a fresh towel to dry your hands from the drawer."

The girls dried their hands on a towel decorated with grapevines that hung from the oven handle, then walked over to the table. The antipasto meats and cheeses tasted delightful and the lasagna was amazing. Martha didn't say another word about the phone, but as shadows swirled around her, she came up with a perfect plan to teach Mia a lesson.

Chapter 17

Trouble in the Temple City

Demas brushed the road dust off the left sitting board of the wagon and motioned for Shoshanna and the other ladies to take a seat. Demas sat opposite his new traveling companions. He made a few comments about the dusty road, hoping to start a conversation, but neither Shoshanna nor the other women commented. While the first woman sensed his eagerness to talk, she determined not to engage the stranger with any further details of her trip. She already thought she had said too much. So while the wagon rolled along, clunking through the worn dirt road, they all kept silent.

Finally, Demas could no longer remain mute, "So, you've met the carpenter?" he asked again.

Shoshanna could not resist talking about the carpenter and softened her stance just a little. "Yes," she answered, glancing up. "I met him in the town where I grew up, not so long ago."

From that point on, Demas peppered her with questions. She gave short answers at first, but she eventually lowered her guard and shared her story. After the exchange, Demas was convinced Shoshanna loved the King and truly believed the carpenter was the Prince. He gathered his courage and repeated his own story, explaining in great detail how the Prince had delivered him from the dragon horde.

By the middle of the afternoon, the two felt like old friends meeting again after a long separation. Neither seemed to notice the hours passing until just outside the city the wagon jolted to a stop.

"This is as far as I can travel with this cart," Thaddeus called to his passengers.

Thousands of people flooded in from all directions, gathering for the feast. Merchants pulled small carts, filled with their wares, shepherds drove flocks through the crowd and in between people scurried trying to avoid crashing into one another. Thaddeus was right, they would have to walk the rest of the way with the pilgrims.

Demas called down to a man gathering up palm branches that littered the way. "Have you seen the one they call the carpenter?"

"Oh yes, he's gone into the city. Caused quite a stir when he came through this way. Everyone is talking about it."

"Thank you," Demas replied.

Demas pulled back the side of his long cloak, revealing a leather purse heavy with silver. He opened it, took out a few coins, and dropped them into the driver's open hand.

"Thank you for the ride, Thaddeus." Then he turned to Shoshanna, "Shall we go toward the temple and look for the Prince?"

"No," she answered. "You are unclean, and I am an outcast. I am afraid our only hope was to catch the Prince before he entered the city for the feast. We'll need to wait outside the city, here among the shops, hoping he returns when the feast is over."

That will be a week or more, or maybe not at all, Demas thought. The other two ladies finally piped up and thanked Demas and the driver for the ride and stepped down off the wagon where they waited for Shoshanna to join them. Demas stood up on the sides of the wagon and scanned the surrounding shops. Then he jumped off the wagon and shouted to Shoshanna, "I have an idea! Follow me."

Against her better judgment, Shoshanna jumped off the wagon and followed the nearly total stranger into the crowded marketplace. Her two traveling companions stood there stunned, then broke their silence with a flurry of critical commentary highlighting their disapproval for Shoshanna's behavior. They bantered back and forth recounting a whole history of foolish mistakes, ending with "When will she ever learn?" They waited in the market for some time but finally continued on their way, agreeing that Shoshanna had likely missed them and would catch up at the prescribed meeting place.

Meanwhile, Demas ran from shop to shop with Shoshanna trailing behind him, trading silver for a new tunic and a long-skirted dress that matched the clothing worn by the pilgrims gathered for the feast. Within a few short minutes, they had traded their worn and dusty garments for the brand-new wardrobe Demas provided. The two shuffled along with the crowd blending in with the pilgrims. No one knew they were foreigners. They traveled through the city gates without a single objection and on to the Temple, where they hoped to find the carpenter.

The outer temple courtyard was wall-to-wall with pilgrims. Demas and Shoshanna wandered through the mass of people for what seemed like hours, hoping to find the Prince or at least hear news of the carpenter's whereabouts. A few folks relayed stories but no one knew his location. Several of the people said remaining at the temple court provided the best chance of finding him, but Shoshanna and Demas already knew that.

Now and again, Demas stood up on his tiptoes and scanned the crowd. Shoshanna wondered what would happen if he did see something. There was simply no way to change locations quickly with so many people blocking the way. But just before dark, as the people began to disburse, Demas grabbed Shoshanna by the hand and pulled her along to the left.

"What do you see?" Shoshanna shouted as she tried to look ahead to figure out what he was aiming for. She couldn't make sense of his actions. Demas seemed to be trying to catch up to two men, both wearing blue striped scarves, decorated with long fringes.

Demas didn't offer an answer, so after they turned a corner and left most of the commotion behind, she tried again. "What do you see?"

"Dragon seed," Demas said as he kept his eyes fixed on the two men.

Dragon seed? Shoshanna wondered what Demas was talking about but then remembered the story he shared with her earlier in the day.

The two men with the scarves hurried up the stone road, meeting a third. He was dressed like the others but was older than either of them. The older man pointed to the left, and all three cut down a narrow street in that direction. Demas made his way up to the corner and peeked around to catch a quick glimpse of the trio just before they turned again and disappeared down another street.

Shoshanna wondered why Demas followed the religious leaders. She had to admit the three looked suspicious—like they were up to something. *Why aren't they in the temple?* she wondered. She quietly tiptoed behind Demas, who was inching up to the second corner but going no further. From here they could easily hear men's voices in discussion. The three leaders were trying to keep quiet, but they were talking much louder than they realized.

"It's done," spoke the first of the men.

"How much did it cost?" the older man questioned.

"What does it matter? As soon as the carpenter is alone tonight, he will signal us."

"Even as we speak, the others are gathering witnesses and preparing them to testify against him," offered the third man, rubbing his hands in expectation.

Demas was right. He knew the look of a man corrupted by the dragon's seed. He imagined that dragons were circling above the three standing around the corner. They were likely celebrating their victory. *Not if I can stop you*, he thought. Again he heard the men speak.

"It would have been a whole lot easier and cheaper if you two would have arrested him in the temple," the older man reprimanded them, shaking his head in frustration.

"What do you propose we would do with the crowd?" the first man spat back harshly. "They'd like to make him king! If we accuse him publicly with no credible witnesses, we will be the ones they stone. Is that what you want?"

"Alright, alright," the older man agreed. "Lower your voice! If his supporters hear us . . . "

But the younger man was not finished chiding his older colleague. "You were not there when the carpenter entered the city. He came in riding on a colt. The gall of the man, posturing himself as the answer to the prophets. He is no king. But that is what they were calling him, you know. He stirred the pilgrims into a frenzy. They cut palm branches, threw down their cloaks for him to tread upon, and cried, 'Hosanna to the King!'"

The older man shrunk back in disbelief.

"It was worth thirty pieces of silver," he reflected, stroking his beard thoughtfully.

"You better hope the usurper shows tonight," the older man shot back. "Arrest him immediately! I want him dead before the feast. Do you understand?"

Demas gasped as the two younger men readily agreed.

"Did you hear that?" the older man asked, holding the back of his right hand to his mouth to signal they should keep quiet.

Demas pivoted around and pulled Shoshanna into a nearby alcove, ducking into the shadows.

Then the older man heard the shuffling of their feet. After a momentary pause, he gave a one-word direction to the two younger men. "Scatter!"

A second later, the older man passed by, retracing his earlier path. Demas waited for a moment, then followed and watched him turn and go right. Easing up to the corner, Demas looked around the rough-cut block to see the older religious ruler walking briskly down the stone road. As Demas turned back to signal Shoshanna, he was startled by a shadowy figure. Before he could react, he was knocked cold to the ground.

Chapter 18

Stuck Behind Bars

When Demas awoke, he felt a throb of pain pulsating from the back of his head. *Where am I? How did I get here?* Little by little, he turned to glanced through an open, barred door. He could see the feet of two soldiers. Demas realized he was lying on the cold stone floor of a prison cell. The musty mildew smell signaled to him that the cell was below ground. He hoped it wasn't a dungeon.

"A victim of a robbery, I suspect," one of the soldiers said breaking the silence.

Demas moved his hands down to feel his left side. His moneybag was gone.

"Why is he here? Why arrest him, Junas?" a second higher-pitched voice questioned.

"Something's amiss. He could be a spy. Underneath his pilgrim tunic, he was dressed as a man from Gadara," Junas said. "He'll be questioned when he wakes. He's lucky to be alive. That was quite a blow he took to the head. Let's finish our check and get out of this hole. It smells of rot and death. I'm ready for some food; it must be close to midday by now."

Demas lay still trying to make sense of things. *Why was he wearing a tunic over his clothes?* He turned his head and spotted a small slit of a window, but as he moved, the cut on the back of his head struck the stone, and he winced. He wanted to cry out but held his tongue, not wanting to alert the guards. Demas heard them close a door and waited till their voices and footsteps faded. Then he let out a groan. *At least this place is only one floor down*, he thought, remembering the window. He reasoned it to be a local holding cell, not a prison.

"Painful, isn't it?" the voice spoke out from the shadows. A chill shot down Demas's spine. He knew that voice but dared not move to look. It was Legion.

"You have no power over me," Demas said still facing away. "I've been set free."

"You say I don't have power over you? How do you think you got here? And as for 'free,' you don't look so free to me. I see that arrogance, boasting, and jealousy cannot grow within your heart, for you've learned to pluck their sprouts before the roots take hold." Legion laughed, spewing dragon seed all across the prison cell. "But let's see how well you do against self-pity, doubt, and unbelief."

"The Son of the King will crush your head!" Demas shot back.

"I don't think so. You failed to warn him, Demas. You should have been there when they arrested him." Legion let out a sickening laugh that echoed off the stone. "Betrayed with a kiss. Mocked, beaten, scourged, and soon he will hang, nailed to a tree. An ironic way for a carpenter to die, wouldn't you say? We've done more than bite against his heel. The dragon horde has already begun celebrating his death."

Demas's heart sank. At that moment, a dragon seed of doubt sprouted, and its root shot down into his heart. Demas struggled against his bindings, trying to break them as he so often did before. But his mind was sound. When the rope bit into his wrist, he winced in pain and stopped struggling. His weakness discouraged him; his hands slumped down, defeated. The root shot deeper still.

Then he remembered how often dragons lied. He shouted back, "You're a liar!" The force of his faith ripped the sprout out before it could take a deeper hold.

"You think I'm lying? You'll see. In a few short hours, the carpenter will die. You'll know we've been successful when the light atop the mountain fades, leaving the lowlands shrouded in darkness." Legion spewed more dragon seed. "I'd love to stay and chat—we've shared such pleasant memories—but I don't want to miss the celebration. When all is dark, I'll come to find you. I'll bring seven even fouler dragons hungry for a home. By that time, your heart will be so twisted with self-pity, you'll welcome us in—just as you did before."

Demas, furious with the dragon, rose to his feet and swung his bound arms, hoping to strike his foe. He missed his mark. The dragon vanished like a wisp of smoke out the narrow slit of the prison window.

While the bindings on his hands were tight, the ropes around his ankles were loose enough that Demas was able to pull free with a little effort. He tossed the ropes to a corner and began to pace in the small cell, trying to remember all that had taken place.

The far past he remembered—his deliverance at the seashore, his restoration to his family. More recent events were fuzzy. He remembered hiring a cart and traveling into the city to warn the Prince. That much was clear. Then he pieced together all he heard from the guards and the few clues that Legion shared. But how did I get into the city? he wondered. *Why am I wearing a tunic, and what happened to . . .* " He paused, then spoke out loud, "Shoshanna?"

Demas rushed to the cell door. "Hey, let me out of here!" he shouted through the flat iron bars. But the guards were gone. They left their post to purchase food, unconcerned that their sole prisoner would escape. Still Demas shouted, "Let me out of here. Hey, is anybody up there?" Then he turned to look toward the window.

There was no way he could reach the small slit, which was at least eight feet off the ground.

Over the course of the next few hours, Demas waited, trying to make sense of the prior evening. He wanted to escape and tried to come up with a plan, but he still could not even free his arms. The guards used such a narrow rope to tie his wrists that he doubted he could have untied the knots even if he'd had his hands free.

When at last he heard the sound of the guards returning, Demas shouted through the bars, "Hello, is anybody up there? Let me out. I've done nothing wrong!"

Demas kept shouting until he heard one of the soldiers walking down the steps. The guard thrust his weight against the door to the lower level, which slammed the stone wall and startled Demas. Once in the central hall below, the guard turned his fury to Demas.

"Shut your mouth!" Junas ordered.

Demas paid the order no mind. "I've done nothing wrong. I demand you release me."

"You demand nothing. If I were you, I'd keep my mouth shut. You are just fortunate you have a friend who's rich enough to bail you out. Mathias and I don't come cheap you know." The guard smiled, revealing a mouthful of yellowed teeth. Then he unlocked the cell and opened the heavy barred door.

*****

As soon as Mrs. Rossi cleared her plate of the last bite, Martha asked, "Can I help you clear the table, Mrs. Rossi?"

"I'll help too," Mia offered, refusing to be upstaged by Martha.

The girls started to clear the plates, load the dishwasher, and wash the pots.

Mrs. Rossi set the lasagna to the side to cool, then put the rest of the food away and started the coffee machine. While the girls worked to finish the last of the dishes, she reset the table for dessert. She brought in a plate piled high with angel wings, generously sprinkled with powdered sugar, and pulled a large tiramisu out of the fridge and set it on the table.

Martha glanced over her shoulder and caught a glimpse of the huge cake. Ever since they were kids, she enjoyed coming over to the Rossis' for dinner, but the desserts—they were the best. Mrs. Rossi grew up in her parents' Italian bakery, so she never, ever served anything but the most amazing desserts.

Martha quickly finished the last of the dishes and turned over the basin filled with soapy water into the sink. Then she wiped off the plastic basin with her washrag and held it above the sink till the last of the water gurgled down the drain. After rinsing out the sink, she placed the plastic basin inside the cabinet below and hung the rag on the faucet, just like Mrs. Rossi always did.

Mia watched and knew she was in for another round of, "Oh, that Martha is such a sweet girl," from her mom as soon as Martha left. She had no idea the conversation would be far worse. Martha was planning a way to expose her plan to go to the party.

Chapter 19

The Dragon's Revenge

"Hold out your hands," the prison guard commanded. Demas gladly obeyed the order. He held up his hands and pulled his wrists as far as he could apart as he could, not wanting the knife to knick his flesh on its way through the ropes. The guard sliced through in a flash. Demas never saw a knife so sharp.

The guard motioned with the knife and said, "Move along and get out of my cell." Demas did his best to tolerate the strong waft of garlic mixed with body odor that assaulted his senses as he obeyed the order.

"Move, I said!" The guard pushed the knife blade into Demas, just hard enough to pierce the skin.

Demas didn't argue. He tossed open the door and ran up the stairs that wound their way up to the ground floor, the rattle of the guard's armor following him up. The stairway opened to a small room where the second soldier sat drinking a beverage.

"Hey, what are you doing out of your cell?" he asked for sport and slammed his fist down on the table. The blow startled Demas, who didn't stay to answer. He sprinted out the open stone doorway and down a set of stairs. Once in the street, he glanced back to the entrance as the guard from below came forward, filling the opening with his bulk.

Demas slipped behind a crowd of people. His mind raced as he once again noticed his missing satchel. He considered questioning the guard regarding his money bag, but thought better of it. Glad to be free but still disoriented, Demas walked on, not sure what to do and trying his best to blend in, despite the gash on the back of his head and the dirt streaking his clothes. He glanced down to the right and could see the slit of a window, which led to the cell below where the guards had held him.

The crowd around Demas scurried off the street to make way for the horses now swiftly approaching. Demas, still focused on the prison's barred window, didn't see them coming. An ox cart rattled its way up the cobblestones from the opposite direction. As Demas turned, he noticed the cart and stepped aside, right into the path of the advancing horses.

"Demas!" Shoshanna shouted and crashed into Demas, slamming them both into the slow-moving cart. The soldier riding the lead horse gave them a disgusted glance; the cart driver adding his rebuke.

Shoshanna grabbed hold of Demas by the shirt and pulled him off the road. The two escaped unharmed.

Safely off the main road, Shoshanna let go of his shirt and brushed him off. "You could have been killed. Are you OK?"

"Yes," he stopped to catch his breath, glancing around in the crowd. "I have a gash back here on my head and I woke up disoriented, but I'll be alright."

"I was afraid they would take the money and then keep you anyway," Shoshanna continued, looking over his wound.

"What happened? How did I get here?"

"Last night, when the religious rulers scattered, I watched you follow the older man into the alcove. The other two younger men left in the opposite direction. I waited behind you in the shadows, thinking you would signal for me to come. Just then, another man with a crazed look on his face crept out of nowhere and hit you with an iron bar. I screamed, and he fled. That is when I ran to you.

"Your head was bleeding, but you were still alive. Two soldiers standing further down the road were alerted by my scream. I heard them coming, so I untied your purse as fast as I could and ran back with it to the alcove. They carried you to the cell. I followed them and waited for them to let you go or for a chance to bail you out. Here is all the money leftover after paying for your release." Shoshanna handed him the near empty leather pouch.

"How did you think to take my money bag?" he asked, amazed at Shoshanna's quick thinking.

"As I told you on the wagon, my past is full of shadows. It is not the first time I've stolen a money bag. If it were not for the carpenter, I would be lost for sure." Tears filled Shoshanna's eyes. "Demas, they've taken him away."

"Taken him? How do you know?"

"Last night I followed the soldiers who carried you here and waited to see if they would release you. I fell asleep over there," Shoshanna pointed to a place where one building jutted out from another, forming a blind corner. "I was awakened by the noise of an angry mob and a squad of guards who brought the carpenter bound down this road. They were taking him to some sort of a trial."

"In the middle of the night? On what charges?"

"They said he was guilty of blasphemy."

Demas pounded his fist. "I had hoped he was lying. I didn't want to believe it."

"Believe what?"

"Legion returned this morning to tempt me," Demas quivered. "Legion spoke of a dragon victory over the carpenter. He said the carpenter had been arrested, beaten, and hung to die on a tree, but I didn't believe him." Demas looked up into the sky, noticing for the first time an increasing darkness, like the dark clouds that roll in before a terrible storm.

Excited to see Demas released, she hadn't noticed the light of day give way to the increasing darkness. Now she too watched the boiling storm above. She had seen fearful, dark green storm clouds before, but these rolling black menaces were far worse.

Without warning, the street beneath their feet began to quake, knocking the two of them to the ground and causing a panic in the city. Fear gripped their hearts and froze them momentarily. Demas remembered the dragon's prophecy. "You'll know we've been successful when the light atop the mountain fades, leaving the lowlands shrouded in darkness." Discouraged beyond measure, a wave of sorrow overwhelmed Demas. He dropped his head to the ground, broke down, and cried.

One horrible thought struck both of them at the same time. The light of the King from atop the mountain was failing. That could only mean one thing—the Prince was dead.

*****

The angel wings were good but the tiramisu was even better. Martha fought to finish the last bite. She was fuller than full but managed to find room for the last piece of ladyfinger daubed with a coating of mascarpone cream.

"Would you like to sleep over, Martha?" Mrs. Rossi asked. "I could swing you home to pick up a few things."

Martha smiled. She had a plan, but this was too easy. Mia, who still had half a slice of cake on her plate, was completely unprepared for Martha's reply. "That is so kind of you, Mrs. Rossi, but I've got church tomorrow and I'll be helping my mom with my grandmother tonight. Also, I don't think my mom would want me to go out with Mia to Derrick's party tonight."

Mia, shocked by Martha's comment, couldn't help herself and blurted out, "Martha!"

Mrs. Rossi gave her daughter a hard stare and spoke sternly, "Who said you were going to a party tonight?"

Martha quickly intervened, "Oh, I'm so sorry. I thought you knew. Mia said everyone knew about Derrick's party."

"I was just thinking about going. I hadn't decided. That's why I didn't get a chance to ask." Mia scrambled for a logical explanation.

Mrs. Rossi could tell when her daughter was lying. "We'll talk about this later," she said, swinging her index finger in Mia's direction.

Mia didn't say another word, but she boiled inside. She was furious with Martha. Martha felt a bit guilty once she saw the glare Mrs. Rossi gave her daughter, but felt justified knowing that she had prevented Mia from getting into far graver trouble.

"I'd better be going. It's getting late," Martha said and walked away from the table. She picked up her backpack and slung it over her right shoulder, then slipped her left arm in. "I'm sorry I can't help you clean up after the dessert. It was amazing, Mrs. Rossi."

Mrs. Rossi smiled and gave Martha a big hug and kissed her cheek.

"Let me drive you home; it will be dark soon," she said.

"Thank you, but it's only a couple of blocks. I'll be fine."

"Alright, then. Don't forget this." Mrs. Rossi turned as she spoke and walked over to the counter. She cut out a large square of lasagna and placed it in an open Tupperware container. After pressing the lid down tight, she walked over and handed it to Martha.

"Mom and Nick will love it," Martha said as she pushed against the screen door, then turned back toward Mia and said, "I'm sorry if I made a mess of things by mentioning the party. I just assumed your mom knew you were going."

"No, don't give it another thought," Mrs. Rossi answered, then turned back to her daughter and added, "I'm sure Mia was just about to ask."

Mrs. Rossi reached over Martha's shoulder and held the door fully open. "Send your mother my love," she said.

"See you later, Mia." Martha stepped down two stairs to the sidewalk below, which she followed around the corner of the house to the driveway. She heard the sound of the back door close firmly. Then as she made her way up the driveway, the explosion began.

"What on earth were you thinking? Do you have no head on your shoulders?"

Martha smiled as she walked. She couldn't make out all the words, but Mrs. Rossi's reprimand continued until she turned the corner of the next block.

Martha didn't gloat too much. Mia really shouldn't be going to parties at Derrick's house. The container of lasagna warmed her hands as the chill of the evening breeze and the rosy sky signaled the closing of the day.

Chapter 20

Victory

T he quake worsened. The stone buildings of the city vibrated.

*****

"Vibrated?" The word jumped off the page and yanked Nick back out of the story as he remembered his phone. He dropped the book, sprang to his feet, and grabbed the phone.

He read the first text, but his heart sank as he continued reading the second. He dropped his head. *Looks like I'll be staying at home*, he thought. Mia was the real reason he wanted to go to the party tonight.

Nick wasn't prepared for the last line of text which read, "& don't ever call again you creep."

What happened? So I missed a few texts? I finally thought I had convinced her to come out to one, he thought.

Shocked and angry, Nick reacted by throwing the phone like a fastball, across the room into the dresser. Instantly it exploded into pieces, the force sent the battery flying out and bouncing across the carpet. He ran to pick up the pieces, hoping to text back but the phone was destroyed. He tossed the pieces back to the floor.

Nick sunk into his beanbag chair trying to make sense of the evening. Why would Mia say that? After sitting quietly for some time, Nick picked up the book and started the chapter over. He wanted a distraction and the book was all he had. The truth was that the story was drawing him in.

*****

The quake worsened. The stone buildings of the city vibrated. Bricks and blocks cracked, punctuating the dull roar that sounded out all around the city. A large decorative stone shook loose from the cornice above Demas and smashed to the ground inches from his head. Shoshanna, who was kneeling on the opposite side trying to encourage Demas, jumped and grabbed hold of his shirt.

"Run!" she shouted as she pulled him up from the cobblestone street and led him down the narrow road toward the open theater in the upper city. The ground gave way before them in waves then rose again, which made it difficult to keep their balance as they ran, now holding onto each other for dear life. People were screaming and flying in all directions.

When they reached the open courtyard, Shoshanna stopped but Demas, who kept on running, yanked her off balance. Shoshanna held her grip and pulled him back. "It is safer here," she said shouting over the rumbling of the earthquake.

Demas didn't know what to do. It seemed to him the world was ending. "The Prince is dead!" he wailed in despair. Tears fell from his eyes. Demas dropped to his knees and shouted up into the pitch-black sky, "I thought he would be the one to set us all free from the curse of the dragon!" As he shouted, a dragon seed of self-pity sprouted and drove a root deep into his heart.

"How do you know he's dead, Demas? He could still be alive," Shoshanna said to encourage him, though she was struggling to believe it herself.

"Can't you see? Look around. The sky is black. The ground beneath our feet is shaking. He's dead, I tell you." Then Demas shouted up into the air, "Why did you bother to come if only to die?"

A foul blast of air hit Demas from above, and he heard a voice speak out, "That's it, Demas. Give in to your anger. Feel the disappointment. The carpenter let you down."

"You! You killed him," Demas shouted up to the dragon, who showed himself as a black shadow against the dark sky. Shoshanna saw nothing. To her, Demas was yelling at an empty sky.

"I didn't kill him. You killed him, Demas. The men of the earth killed him. He came to rescue you, but he failed. Humanity is hopeless to fight against the seed of the dragon. We rule the world now. We are the mighty dragons!"

Demas hung his head; there was no use fighting. *It's all over*, he thought.

The dragon continued his assault, "Look at you! You who were once delivered have fallen again. There is no carpenter to save you this time," Legion said, then howled with delight. "Feel the roots go deep. You can't stop them because there is nothing left to live for. See above? Look up, Demas. See for yourself. The light atop the mountain is black as night. Give in, Demas. Join forces with me again. Welcome me in."

Self-pity in Demas turned to doubt. Doubt gave way to unbelief and unbelief to anger as the dragon roots shot down deeper still into the battered man's heart. "Everything is lost," he said and gave up resisting the dragon.

Shoshanna heard his last few words and watched her friend collapse. Off in the distance, a cloud parted for a moment, just enough to show Shoshanna a glimmer of light.

"No!" she cried and reached down to grab Demas by the arm. She turned him over and looked into his eyes. "He is a liar, Demas. Don't listen to him." She embraced Demas and with all her strength she held onto him. "Fight," she cried. "Fight!"

Her words penetrated to the core of his heart, slowing the growth of the dragon roots. Demas felt a wave of hope swell within his heart. "The carpenter may be dead," he said and continued, each word louder than the one before, "But—I—will—not—give—in to the dragon." Demas lifted his weight, then drew to his knees. He repeated himself as he stood tall. "I will not give in to the dragon." With renewed strength he shouted into the black sky, "You are a liar! I will never bow to you! The words of the Prince are still true! And whether he's still here or not, he has rescued me forever!" Then he commanded the dragon with the same authority the carpenter displayed, "In the name of the Prince, be gone, you dragon filth, be gone!"

The command struck a mighty blow to the dastardly reptile, who tumbled backward out of control as if struck by a locomotive. The usurper screamed in pain and was cast away in an instant. The last rumble of the earthquake sounded, then all grew quiet and still. Demas turned to Shoshanna. "It was Legion," he said.

"I know," Shoshanna said. "But he's gone."

"No, it is more than that. Something has changed," Demas said as he replayed the last few minutes over in his mind. "Legion's hold was broken by the power of the Prince in me. The moment I resisted in his name, Legion fled."

"You stood against him in the power of the Prince. Legion is no match for the Prince," she said to encourage him.

Then Demas took Shoshanna's hand and pulled her toward him. "Thank you," he said from the core of his being. "When I was at my weakest, you were there to give me strength."

Shoshanna smiled. "You're welcome, but it is the Prince who gives us both strength." And she held his hand between her own. "What do we do now?"

"I don't know. Go home?" He paused, then added, "I'm not sure."

They stood there stunned by the destruction around them. All about them people crept out of hiding now that the quake had calmed. Voices called out for loved ones, some in fear, while others rejoiced as they found that family members and friends were safe.

"Well," she thought aloud, "Unless you want to walk, we'll need to wait in the city for a few days. The cart drivers will not be working on the Sabbath, and the fee will be far too expensive early Sunday morning. Everyone's going to want to clear out of the city after all that has happened today."

"I can cover the fee," Demas said. Then reached down to grab his purse.

Shoshanna smiled, then let a short laugh slip out when she saw him pull up the near-empty money bag. Demas laughed as well. "I guess we'll wait until Monday," he said.

"Come with me," Shoshanna offered as she pulled him by the hand. "I have friends who live outside the city. I planned to spend the night there with my village companions. I'm sure they are worried. I hope they're safe. You can join us there for a few days. If we leave now, we can make it through the gate without much trouble."

Demas, shaken and sorrowful from the day's events, did not object. His weary soul needed a safe place to rest and come to terms with all that had happened.

Shoshanna led the way. As they walked, gratefulness for Shoshanna swelled in Demas's heart. Her confidence strengthened him. This thought occupied him until they reached the city gate where a group of men were discussing the night's events.

"Yes, they hung him on a tree!" one man shouted across the crowd to another, eager to hear the news.

"Do you think the quake was a sign?" the man across the street inquired.

"Coincidence is all. Though I admit it is a bit eerie."

"I think it was a sign—from the King of the Mountain.

"A sign that he was a fraud!" someone else shouted.

"He saved others, but he couldn't save himself."

"All hail the King . . . of the dead," another mocker added.

Demas shivered and pulled Shoshanna through the crowd, glad to get beyond the gate. Then Shoshanna led them through a maze of shops and tents and a row of clay brick homes. Several of the crude brick structures were collapsed from the shaking. Demas followed her through the unfamiliar marketplace, ducking the merchandise that hung along the way. Though it was late, people everywhere filled the streets, afraid a second quake could come at any minute.

An older merchant woman backed out into the street in front of them, her attention focused on a hole in the wall above where several bricks had fallen and crashed down upon her wares. As they zigzagged their way down the stone alleys avoiding many such scenes, Demas wrestled through the day's events. He remembered how decisively his command dispelled the dragon. *Something is different*, he thought to himself. *I've never experienced such confidence, such faith.*

"We're almost there," Shoshanna said. Then as they turned the next corner, passing a makeshift corral where two mules were tied, she pointed. "There it is."

The well-built home ahead of them stood strong, unfazed by the quake. Shoshanna ran across the street to the door. She knocked and called out to her friend, "Mary, it's Shoshanna." Mary recognized her voice and raced to let her in. The friend's smile faded when she caught sight of Demas.

"He's a trustworthy friend," Shoshanna quickly reassured the woman. "He, too, has had a lifesaving encounter with the Prince. We were caught in the city during the shaking. I told him this would be a safe place to stay until the city empties."

Mary's smile returned, and she welcomed the two of them inside, where Shoshanna embraced her concerned village friends who were sure to pull her aside to scold her for deserting them the day before.

Demas looked about the place. His shoulders relaxed. The scent of spices filled the air. The house felt like home with sheepskins covering the floor in the main room. Soon Mary's husband

Nathaniel returned from the market with fresh vegetables and meat for stew.

The warm, albeit muted conversation that followed dinner brought a welcome distraction from the day's events for everyone concerned. Demas discovered that Mary and Shoshanna grew up together in the same village with the other two ladies until Mary and her husband moved to the city to establish their market shop. Picking up on a few discrete comments, Demas learned that Shoshanna had lived a hard and broken life. She hadn't revealed all the details of her challenges when they first met. She had only said that she was an outcast welcomed by the Prince.

Time passed as they exchanged stories late into the evening, each steering clear of more recent events. When eventually the topic could not be avoided, they expressed their sorrow and disappointment at the carpenter's demise. Soon after, the conversation stalled as everyone was tired and ready for bed. Shoshanna and her traveling companions settled in a side room. Mary tossed a blanket to Demas who lay down on the front room floor. He doubled up a sheepskin for a pillow and sank into a pool of soft wool, sleeping through the night.

Chapter 21

A Return to the Well

Demas slept late into the next day, glad for the rest. Nathaniel led him on a tour of the neighborhood, greeting friends and surveying the damage from the earthquake. The day passed quickly as Demas and Shoshanna joined Nathaniel and Mary, along with the others, to help a neighbor whose storage room collapsed on one of his livestock. After working to rescue the animal, everyone slept soundly.

Demas woke up earlier the second morning to the repeated call of a rooster. Glad for the hospitality, but eager to get on the road, he left in search of a driver and cart. It was time to go home. He stopped at the stable close to Nathaniel's and soon discovered that Shoshanna had been right about transport on Sunday. Laurentia, the wife of the stable owner confirmed that the drivers were still charging double.

But by evening, the rush of pilgrims leaving the city slowed. The drivers, back to competing for the few remaining travelers, were all too glad to lower their prices. Demas negotiated a reasonable fare for the four of them with a driver named Tymar. Tymar agreed to an even lower fare if they were willing to share the cart with several goats, left over from the celebration. Tymar took the deposit Demas earlier collected from the others. He would give the driver the balance once he reached home.

After saying their goodbyes, the four travelers walked over to the cart, which stopped at the stable to fill the feedbags. Shoshanna didn't mind the tight quarters of the wagon half-filled with cages as it forced her to sit closer to Demas. She wanted to be careful, but her feelings for him were undeniable and growing stronger. She had allowed her emotions toward men to race far ahead of wisdom too many times. Ever since meeting the carpenter, however, she had left that lifestyle, along with a craving for affection, and lived alone. These feelings left her confused, though, for they seemed different and she didn't know what to do about them.

Demas too felt drawn to Shoshanna. He couldn't imagine going back home without her, but thought it crazier still that she would ever be interested in his pursuit. He felt unworthy to be married. After all, he spent half of his life crazed, living among the tombs. He was not husband material.

*****

Nick's eyes began to well with tears. He had felt alone for so long, encased by his hardened shell of resentment. He thought of the dragon seed that he now knew had been sprouting in his own heart and looked down at the ball he had absently stuck in his pocket.

His dad's golf ball.

Nick set the book aside, pulled the ball from his pocket, and closed his eyes. He remembered the first time his father told him the story of the special ball as if it were yesterday.

"God saved my life, and it all started with this little golf ball," his father said, standing in front of the fireplace, pulling the ball off the mantel stand and showing it to his son. "Before I met your mom, I would go golfing with your uncle Dennis. I learned a lot from him. He was always such a great teacher, but he was always trying to get me to go to church. We were on the back nine, just finished hole seventeen. As we traveled to eighteen, he started in again, trying to convince me that I needed God. I just laughed. I rifled through the pouch on the side of my bag and pulled out a brand-new Ping Eye; this very one. As I teed it up I shouted, "The day I get a hole in one, that'll be the day I'll go with you to church."

"I moved up to the ball, took a practice swing or two with my seven iron and swung for the green. I sliced the ball good and laughed as it curved for the trees. *No church for me*, I thought. But before I could say a word, I heard a loud pop and watched my ball bounce off a large rock and shoot back at the green. It rolled up to the pin and dropped straight into the hole! I was so excited I jumped and screamed, then remembered my words to Dennis. That Sunday I went to church. It only took one message for the Holy Spirit to show me that I need saving—before that I hadn't really thought that I did anything wrong. But hearing the pastor speak about how self-centered he was and how much he needed Jesus made me realize that I was just the same. Later, as much as I wanted to boast in that hole-in-one, I couldn't. I couldn't tell the story without talking about the rock. I know that I didn't get the hole-in-one, he did."

Nick cried as he remembered his dad handing him the ball and pointing to the scar left on the ball from where it hit the rock. A year after his father first told Nick the story, he was diagnosed with liver cancer. It robbed him of life a month later. Nick hated that God took his dad away and couldn't bear looking at that ball sitting up on its stand in the center of the mantel. So one day he took it and hid it in his desk drawer. The worst part was when his mother noticed the treasured memento was missing. When she had asked him about it, he had denied any knowledge of the ball's whereabouts. It was yet one more act of deceit he had piled onto his record. He now wanted to tell her that he was the one who had taken the golf ball.

Nick looked down at the book. He was almost through. He picked it up and started reading again.

*****

The driver took the route through Sychar, which passed by a large well. As he approached the well, the traffic slowed. Tymar pulled off to wait in line with the other carts and shepherds for water. The spaces between the wagons were crammed with people and animals moving to and from the well. The high-pitched bleats of goats and sheep thirsty for water, along with the bells on the cattle, played like a shepherd's symphony. The squeak of cart wheels and murmur of the crowd added background accompaniment. Shouting over it all, Tymar called to a group of boys, who came bursting through the crowd to the cart with waterskins so full they looked as if they could pop. He paid a young lad a few pennies, and at once the cart was swarming with children filling the small troughs in the cages.

Shoshanna stood up from her seat to say goodbye. "I can't deny my deep sadness over the events of the last few days. And yet I am grateful for the opportunity to have met a new friend." She smiled and held out her hand. "Will you consider me a friend?"

"A friend? Yes, of course," Demas answered, and held her hand between both of his. He wanted to say so much more, but instead he only added, "Goodbye, Shoshanna." And then, "Allow me to assist you all."

Demas jumped off the cart and extended his hand. Shoshanna's friends stepped down first and seemed glad to take his hand to aid them. Then Shoshanna took his hand. She held it tightly as she stepped off the cart onto the side rail and then down to the ground. Once ushering her safely down, he pulled his hand from hers—how he hated letting go! Demas climbed back aboard the cart and tapped the driver on the shoulder to let him know he was ready to depart. The driver snapped the reins and the cart jolted to a start. Shoshanna watched with tears streaming down her face as the cart rode away with fits and starts, working its way through the crowded road. Her traveling companions melted into the crowd, but she stood watching the cart drive away.

"You should run after him," a voice sounded from her left.

"That is what I feel, but I'm just . . . " Shoshanna didn't finish her answer. She stared ahead, not wanting to take her eyes off Demas as his cart mixed in with the traffic leaving the city.

"Here, have a drink," the stranger said and handed her a cup filled with water.

Shoshanna looked down at the cup and noticed a scar on the back of the stranger's hand.

"Go on, have a drink," the man said as he placed the cup in her grasp.

"The well is deep, and you have nothing to draw water with."

Shoshanna snapped her head around toward the man in disbelief, for she recognized his voice. "You're alive!" she said. Her eyes popped open wide.

"Yes, I am very much alive, Shoshanna." Then he pointed to the cart. "If you run now, you'll catch him," he said waving his hand in that direction.

Shoshanna turned again to look for Demas. She could still see his cart, caught in the jam on the road. She turned to the carpenter and started to say, "But . . . "

The carpenter smiled. "Go on. You are forgiven," he said. With those words, a warmth rushed through her body straight to Shoshanna's heart. Without another word, she took off running, shouting as she ran. She dodged a small mob of sheep and slipped ahead of an older fellow, listing back and forth as he sauntered down the road. As she approached the wagon, she shouted out again to Demas, "He's alive! He's alive!"

Chapter 22

The Revelation

Nick dropped the book to his lap. He couldn't help but repeat the words he just read, "He's alive. He's alive." The phrase stirred something deep inside of him. He wanted to jump and run, but he wanted to finish the last chapter even more, so he buckled down, blew out a deep breath and continued reading.

*****

Dear reader, thank you for traveling with me this far. My father first told me this story after my fourteenth birthday. At the time, the dragon seed of pride filled my heart with black twisted roots. If it were not for the topic of dragons, I don't think I would have listened to his words. The tale of the dragons helped me hear the story behind the story. If you've made it this far, then you too must now realize the true identity of the carpenter. He is Jesus.

Now lest you think the dragon is a made-up character from a fable, let me share with you the story as spoken by the apostle John.

> *Now war arose in heaven, Michael and his angels fighting against the dragon. And the dragon and his angels fought back, but he was defeated, and there was no longer any place*

for them in heaven. And the great dragon was thrown down, that ancient serpent, who is called the devil and Satan, the deceiver of the whole world—he was thrown down to the earth, and his angels were thrown down with him. And I heard a loud voice in heaven, saying, "Now the salvation and the power and the kingdom of our God and the authority of his Christ have come, for the accuser of our brothers has been thrown down, who accuses them day and night before our God. And they have conquered him by the blood of the Lamb and by the word of their testimony, for they loved not their lives even unto death. Therefore, rejoice, O heavens and you who dwell in them! But woe to you, O earth and sea, for the devil has come down to you in great wrath, because he knows that his time is short!"

And when the dragon saw that he had been thrown down to the earth, he pursued the woman who had given birth to the male child. But the woman was given the two wings of the great eagle so that she might fly from the serpent into the wilderness, to the place where she is to be nourished for a time, and times, and half a time. The serpent poured water like a river out of his mouth after the woman, to sweep her away with a flood. But the earth came to the help of the woman, and the earth opened its mouth and swallowed the river that the dragon had poured from his mouth. Then the dragon became furious with the woman and went off to make war on the rest of her offspring, on those who keep the commandments of God and hold to the testimony of Jesus. And he stood on the sand of the sea. (Revelation 12:7–17)

So you see, the dragon is very real and means to make war against every one of us. Unfortunately, our first far-off grandparents, Adam and Eve, gave into the temptation of the dragon and rebelled against

God. Since that day, the terrible sin of pride, which is rebellion against God, was passed down to each of us. We are all born with sin, and we are helplessly lost in our sin.

But none of this took God by surprise. Even before the creation of the world, he planned to save his children by sending his only Son to take our punishment. Given the name Jesus, the Son of God lived a perfect, sinless life as a carpenter and never gave in to pride.

When the time was right, he began to push back the curse of sin by healing the sick and casting out the dragon from those he possessed—and yes, even from the two men of Gadara. Matthew spoke of them in the eighth chapter of his Gospel, verse twenty-eight.

Jealous of his authority and power, sinful men sentenced him to death and nailed him to a cross. To mock him, they gave him a crown of thorns and hung a sign above his head, which read, "This is the King of the Jews." While Jesus hung suffering upon the cross, something even more terrible took place. God his Father and the King of Heaven punished Jesus for our sin. Jesus willingly took our punishment to restore our relationship with God and break the dragon's hold over us.

Because Jesus lived a perfect, sinless life, death could not hold him in the grave. On the third day, Jesus rose again, bursting forth from the tomb in glorious power. He appeared to over 500 of his followers to prove that he indeed rose from the dead. Before returning to heaven, Jesus promised to send his Holy Spirit to live in the hearts of every person who believes in him.

Today when people who are dead in their sin hear this gospel story, the Holy Spirit touches them to bring them back to life. Once alive again, our stony hearts soften and the dragon roots of pride begin to shrivel up and die, and we are set free to believe in Jesus. Then Jesus, by his Spirit, comes to live inside us and gives each of us the power to resist the dragon and cause him to flee. No one can win the fight against the dragon's temptations on his own without the Spirit's power. Our salvation and forgiveness from sin come to us through trusting in Jesus alone.

So what about you? Remember, the antidote to the sinful dragon seed of pride is humility. So will you humble yourself and admit your sin? Will you turn from it and run to Jesus, the Prince of Peace, and be set free? Now is the time for you to ask the Prince to pluck out the dragon roots within your heart. Do not miss the opportunity to humble yourself and cry out to God for help.

Beware of pride—it turns the wisest into fools. Children grow up hating their parents because of their pride. Husbands leave their wives and wives leave their husbands all because they refuse to follow God's plan and instead follow their own. People refuse to forgive; in their pride they keep a list of other people's wrongs. Anger and bitterness consume them. Pride deceived the dragon into thinking he won a victory at the cross. That is how blind we become in our pride. Dragon seed, twisting its roots deep in our hearts, can fool us into thinking we are winning when we are actually losing everything. Our only hope is to turn away from pride and Satan, that dragon of old, and turn to Jesus to save and set us free.

Though Christ defeated Satan at the cross and sealed our victory by rising from the dead, the Dragon and his horde still roam the earth. Like a crazed lunatic, Satan spreads his lies, hoping to deceive the children of man. Even after God saves us from the dragon, the battle rages on. But Jesus gave us this promise: One day he will return to defeat the dragon for all time and lock him in the abyss. The dragon's days are numbered; his end God has foretold. I leave you with this word of prophecy:

> Then I saw an angel coming down from heaven, holding in his hand the key to the bottomless pit and a great chain. And he seized the dragon, that ancient serpent, who is the devil

and Satan, and bound him for a thousand years, and threw him into the pit, and shut it and sealed it over him, so that he might not deceive the nations any longer, until the thousand years were ended. After that he must be released for a little while.

Then I saw thrones, and seated on them were those to whom the authority to judge was committed. Also I saw the souls of those who had been beheaded for the testimony of Jesus and for the word of God, and those who had not worshiped the beast or its image and had not received its mark on their foreheads or their hands. They came to life and reigned with Christ for a thousand years. The rest of the dead did not come to life until the thousand years were ended. This is the first resurrection. Blessed and holy is the one who shares in the first resurrection! Over such the second death has no power, but they will be priests of God and of Christ, and they will reign with him for a thousand years.

And when the thousand years are ended, Satan will be released from his prison and will come out to deceive the nations that are at the four corners of the earth, Gog and Magog, to gather them for battle; their number is like the sand of the sea. And they marched up over the broad plain of the earth and surrounded the camp of the saints and the beloved city, but fire came down from heaven and consumed them, and the devil who had deceived them was thrown into the lake of fire and sulfur where the beast and the false prophet were, and they will be tormented day and night forever and ever. (Revelation 20:1–10)

Chapter 23

The End of the Story

*O*h yes, I almost forgot to finish the story. I am sure you are curious about Demas and Shoshanna.

*****

With permission from the carpenter, Shoshanna took off running to catch up with Demas, yelling all the way up the road, "He's alive! He's alive!" When she finally reached the wagon, out of breath, she tried to speak but could only mumble through mingled sobs and tears.

Demas didn't know what she was talking about, but the sight of Shoshanna triggered his emotions and he too began to cry. Demas jumped off the wagon and took Shoshanna in his arms. They embraced for a moment before Shoshanna pulled away to tell Demas about her encounter at the well.

The two of them raced back to see if they could find the Prince. Tymar, who had been listening to their conversation as they drove along the road, wanted to meet the carpenter too. So he jumped off and left his wagon in the jam—which didn't help traffic much that day—and followed close behind.

Shoshanna led them to the same spot at the well, but the Prince was gone. Demas didn't make the same mistake twice. This time, he invited Shoshanna to travel home with him. Shoshanna brimmed with joy as she traveled with Demas toward Gadara. They were soon married and dedicated their lives to spreading the story about the Prince and all that he did for each of them.

In time, they had a son, who became their greatest earthly joy. As their boy grew older, the dragon horde did all they could to tempt him and turn him against Demas and Shoshanna. While the carpenter did die to break the curse, every son or daughter born to man must believe for himself.

So the dragon horde went after the young lad, tempting him with the dragon seed of pride. When Demas saw his son giving in to disrespect and refusing to humble himself, he knew it was time to share the whole story with his son. Up until then, Demas had kept secret the unpleasant details of his former life, living in the tombs, possessed by the dragons.

The story helped his son recognize the hold of dragon seed upon his own heart. He turned from his sin and believed in the carpenter Prince, the Son of the King, who broke the power of evil and set him free. At that moment, the dragon roots growing in the boy's heart were dissolved to nothing.

Oh, and there is one more thing to tell. There is a tradition that has carried on from that time until today. Through the years, each firstborn son or daughter has always been named after a character in the story. In that way, it is believed, the story of the carpenter will come to life for each successive generation. It all started with Demas, or should I say, Nicodemus, who named his son Thad, after Thaddeus, the cart driver who drove Demas and Shoshanna to the city. Thad in turn, carried on the tradition his father started by naming his firstborn daughter after her grandmother, but he loved to call her Anna.

So now you know all there is to tell, and you have a choice to make. You can give yourself to pride, be captured by the dragon, and ruled by the power of the dragon seed sprouting in your heart.

Or, you can turn from your pride and place your trust in Jesus, the carpenter, the Prince of Peace, who died to set you free.

*****

Nick knew what he must do. He dropped the book and cried out for forgiveness. At once the dragon roots that had burrowed deep into his heart were uprooted. Nick raced to the family room with tears streaming down his face. He pulled out the ball from his pocket and placed it back on the stand where it belonged. His mother and grandmother looked up and their eyes too filled with tears. Nick pulled his mom up from her chair and held her tight, sobbing.

"I'm sorry. I'm so sorry, Mom," Nick said, his body shaking with emotion.

Nick and his mom held each other for quite some time, their tight embrace spoke a thousand words. Then Nick turned to his grandmother.

"I'm sorry to you too, Mom-Mom," he sniffed. Then asked his grandmother a question.

"Mom-Mom, what is your full name?"

His grandmother smiled. "I've been hoping one day you would ask. It's Shoshanna," she replied.

Just then Martha rounded the corner, returning from her friend's house. Martha took in the teary scene before them and noticed that the ball was suddenly back in place on the mantel.

It figures, she sulked. *I hope he doesn't think returning that ball makes up for all the trouble he's caused.*

A shadow swirled about her.

The Antidote

The secret to uprooting the seed of the dragon.

A twelve-day prescription.

Day One

The First Law of Pride

God opposes the proud, but gives grace to the humble.

James 4:6

You can do some fun experiments with gravity. If you drop a marble or small pebble in a glass of water, it will always fall to the bottom. The force of gravity in the earth's core pulls the marble down because it is heavier than the water. Scientists use the word "law" to describe the way gravity works because it always works the same way. Drop a million marbles in a million glasses of water and every one will sink. That is because God designed the world we live in to operate under laws like the law of gravity.

There are also spiritual laws that govern our lives. One of these spiritual laws is that "God opposes the proud but gives grace to the humble" (James 4:6). Think about that: If you are proud, God will be against you. That's a spiritual law that will always be true, no matter what. Since God made us and is in charge of the whole world, it would make sense to figure out what pride is and how to get rid of it. So what does James mean by pride? It's simply wanting to be in charge of our lives instead of acknowledging that God is really in charge.

Our enemy, the one the Bible calls "The Dragon, that ancient serpent, who is the devil and Satan" (Revelation 20:2) is always ready to tempt us toward pride. The Dragon is very aware that we are sinners who can be tempted to turn away from God and live for ourselves. Any time we live for ourselves and do what we want over what God wants or any time we boast in our own glory instead of giving God the glory we can be sure that sinful pride is active in our heart, sprouting and growing like the dragon seed of the story.

Sinful pride is at work whenever we reject God's Word and do what we want instead. When we tell lies, we are rejecting God's direction to tell the truth. When we take something that doesn't belong to us, pride is at work because we are following our selfish desire and making it more important than God's Word, which tells us not to steal. Pride is at work behind the scenes with every sin. That is why God opposes the proud.

God is perfect. There is no sin in him at all. He is completely good and holy. That is why he must oppose sin. We would expect a police officer to chase down a robber and arrest him for taking a lady's purse. By doing so he is protecting us. We would expect a judge to find him guilty. That would be just. In the same way, God must go after lawbreakers and judge them.

Since we are all proud, you might be wondering what hope is there? But James give us the way forward—humility. Humility is the opposite of pride. Pride is lifting ourselves above God, but humility is embracing our rightful place below him and accepting that God is in charge of our lives and not us. Humility is like when a person bows before the throne of their king. Bowing symbolizes submission. It says to the King, "I am your subject. You are in authority over me." Likewise, whenever we obey God's word instead of our own sinful desires, we bow before the Lord in our hearts. That's what humbling ourselves means. If we do that, James tells us that God will help us by giving us grace. What does this mean practically? Among other things, when you obey God's

Word by obeying your parents even when you don't feel like it—that's humility. And God gives grace to the humble!

What does grace look like? It's help from God to do what he asks us to do. God's grace helps us to do something hard even though every part of us wants to say *No!* But God's grace also means that whenever you ask for forgiveness in Jesus's name, you are forgiven. God never holds our sins against us when we confess them and ask for his help. Can you think of any sins that you might want to confess and be forgiven for?

Just like the law of gravity is constant and never changes, so God will always oppose the proud, and he will always give grace to the humble.

Look for opportunities to walk the path of humility. Think about your relationship with your parents and your teachers. Is it hard for you to take direction? Ask Jesus to help you walk in humility with those in authority over you. What are some ways you can express yourself that show humility instead of pride? God promises that if you do, it will go well for you and you will live a long life (Ephesians 6:2–3).

WHAT ABOUT YOU?

1. Usually we are blind to the work of pride in our lives. Have you ever asked someone where they see pride at work in your life? If you were to ask someone this question, who would you ask? Who knows you best?

2. Where in your life do you see pride at work? In other words, where do you do what you want to do instead of what you know God wants you to do? Make a short list and share that with someone else so that you can pray for each other.

Day Two

The Second Law of Pride

Pride goes before destruction, and a haughty spirit before a fall.
Proverbs 16:18

Most mountain climbers use a harness, ropes, and tackle to climb. They use ropes because mountain climbing is dangerous, and it is easy to make a mistake. But if you secure yourself to the rock with a rope, and you lose your grip and fall, the rope becomes a safety line to hold you and keep you from falling. If your rope is attached correctly to the rock, then the rock you are climbing becomes your salvation.

The more dangerous the climb, the more important it is to use ropes. But some climbers have attempted some of the world's most difficult cliffs without any ropes at all, trusting their own strength to save them. They know if they slip, they fall to their death, crashing on the rocks below. So why would anyone try to climb a 300-foot-high wall of jagged rock without the safety of a harness, against the counsel of other experienced climbers? The answer is one word: pride.

Pride tells us we can live life on our own without the help of others (or ropes in the case of our risky climber). Pride tells us that we don't need our parents' advice or help; that we know better.

Pride tells us that we don't need our teacher's help; we can do it on our own. Pride steers us away from God and his Word. Pride tells us that we will never fall. What is the second law of pride? Proverbs 16:18 says it clearly—if you are proud, you will fall!

In the book of Isaiah, you can read about one of the greatest falls from the heights of pride—the story of Day Star, son of the Dawn. Bible scholars believe this could be an illusion to the fall of Satan who turned against God and convinced a company of angels to rebel with him. Deceived by his pride, he thought he could rule as God. It is funny how pride deceives us into believing we can do anything. But the Day Star was wrong and was cast down into the pit of Sheol.

> How you are fallen from heaven,
>   O Day Star, son of Dawn!
> How you are cut down to the ground,
>   you who laid the nations low!
> You said in your heart,
>   "I will ascend to heaven;
> above the stars of God
>   I will set my throne on high;
> I will sit on the mount of assembly
>   in the far reaches of the north;
> I will ascend above the heights of the clouds;
>   I will make myself like the Most High."
> But you are brought down to Sheol,
>   to the far reaches of the pit. (Isaiah 14:12–15)

Pride will try to fool you into thinking you will be the one person who doesn't fall. Let the Word of God and the wise counsel of those who listen to God be the harness and ropes that keep you tied close to God, who is your rock.

Remember that old Dragon will always try to fool you. Here are a few of his lies: No one will ever know. You won't get caught.

You can stop whenever you want. If you hear these lies, fight them with the truth of God's Word. "Whoever sows to please their flesh, from the flesh will reap destruction" (Galatians 6:8 NIV). "Pride goes before destruction, and a haughty spirit before a fall" (Proverbs 16:18).

WHAT ABOUT YOU?

1. Can you think of a time where you were too stubborn to ask for help because you thought you could do it on your own?

2. God places people in our lives to act like the ropes of a mountain climber. They are there to keep us from falling or doing something unwise. Who are the people God has place in your life to keep you from falling into trouble?

3. Are you using those folks or free climbing without their help? Think of some practical ways you could ask for help.

Day Three

The Power of Desire

Blessed is the man who remains steadfast under trial, for when he has stood the test he will receive the crown of life, which God has promised to those who love him. Let no one say when he is tempted, "I am being tempted by God," for God cannot be tempted with evil, and he himself tempts no one. But each person is tempted when he is lured and enticed by his own desire. Then desire when it has conceived gives birth to sin, and sin when it is fully grown brings forth death.

James 1:12–15

A plate of warm chocolate cookies sitting out on a table will tempt even the most obedient child to take one. Imagine a little girl, staring at that plate of cookies, drawing in the chocolate scented steam, as her mother says, "Honey, I've got to go into my bedroom to change my clothes. Don't touch the cookies. They are for our guests."

While her mom's instruction is simple and clear, it is not so easy to obey. For deep inside our heart pride says, "Don't do what is best for others, do what is best for you." With sin on the inside and the aroma of freshly baked cookies on the outside, the little girl in our story is lured by her own desire. Her mom said, "Do not touch" but her desire tells her, "Just take one."

Here is the question: Will she say no to her desire and obey her mom? Or give into her desire and disobey? The desire to eat a warm cookie is not wrong. But when her mom has said no, that desire fuels the temptation to disobey.

You can be sure that whenever we experience temptation, the pride in our heart goes to work overtime to give us a thousand reasons why we can do what we want, instead of doing what is right. Here are just a few thoughts the young girl in the example might be facing as temptations to get her to follow her sinful desire and disobey:

> You can take one cookie, there is a whole plate full.
> Nobody will miss one cookie.
> One cookie won't spoil your appetite.
> You will be able to eat one later, so why not now?
> Your mom will never know you took one.
> There are too many to fit on the plate, so eating one could help.
> You are old enough to make this decision on your own.
> It is better to eat them now while they are warm.

Perhaps you can remember a time in your life when you gave in to temptation. You might say, "What is the big deal with eating a cookie?" It is not likely that eating a forbidden cookie will lead to death, but James warns us for good reason in today's Bible passage.

God must punish sin, even one single sin, and the punishment for sin is death. So while any one sin might not seem so bad, it is always a foolish choice to sin. Even one sin separates us from our God and places us under his judgment. That might seem like the worst news ever (and it is), because no one can resist all temptations. I don't know about you, but I struggle with way worse temptations than eating a warm cookie.

Do you remember the temptation Satan spoke through the serpent to the woman in the garden of Eden? Satan twisted God's words and convinced Eve to eat the forbidden fruit. Instead of doing what she knew to be right, she was deceived by his temptations. Eve's disobedience and that of her husband opened the door for sin to enter the world. Ever since then, every man, woman, and child is under the curse of sin.

The truth is that none of us can do the right thing all the time. Deep down inside we are sinners and need God's help to change. We can't do the right thing without God's help. When we place our trust in God and his plan of salvation through Jesus Christ's death on the cross, he forgives us and places his Holy Spirit into our hearts to help us. Only with the help of the Holy Spirit can we say no to sin and yes to God's plan for our lives.

Living for God brings life. Solomon, the wisest man who ever lived said it this way: "In the path of righteousness is life, and in its pathway there is no death" (Proverbs 12:28).

So what about you? Which path will you choose?

WHAT ABOUT YOU?

1. Where are you most tempted to sin in your life?

2. Can you remember a temptation that came to you but you said no? What did it feel like to say no to sin?

3. The single most important piece of information to know is the gospel—the good news that God sent his Son Jesus into the world. Look up Colossians 2:13–14 and write down why God sent his Son.

Day Four

Who Will Represent You?

Therefore, just as sin came into the world through one man, and death through sin, and so death spread to all men because all sinned—for sin indeed was in the world before the law was given, but sin is not counted where there is no law. Yet death reigned from Adam to Moses, even over those whose sinning was not like the transgression of Adam, who was a type of the one who was to come.

Romans 5:12–14

The United States elects a president every four years. Six months before the election, the Republicans and Democrats choose a candidate to represent their party in the election. If the Democratic candidate wins the election, the whole Democratic Party also wins, for he was their representative. They then staff the government with Democrats. If the Republican candidate wins, so does the Republican Party. The outcome of the election for each of these parties often depends on how well the one person does.

In a similar way, the very first man, created by God, was the representative for all people. If Adam obeyed God and refused to eat from the forbidden tree, he would live forever free from sin, enjoying God, and so would all his children. If Adam disobeyed, death and sin would enter the human race and be passed on to every child born.

Sadly, Adam disobeyed and passed his sin on to all of us. That is what the passage from Romans describes. Sin and death came into the world through one man. We are all born sinners because Adam, our far-off grandfather, disobeyed. As a result, every one of us sins.

Think of your life: Have you ever told a lie? Have you ever taken something that did not belong to you? Have you ever spoken disrespectfully to your parents? Do you fight with your siblings? Do you ever forget to keep God as the number one priority of your life and worship him?

We've already talked about how the punishment for even one sin is death. But God still loved Adam and Eve, so he gave them a promise. One day, a son of Adam would stand as a new representative head. Just as through one man, sin came to all, so through this one man righteousness would come.

The man who came to represent us was Jesus. God sent his Son to be born a man into a family in the line of Adam. But Adam's sin did not pass to Jesus, for the Holy Spirit put him in the womb of Mary before her marriage to Joseph. Joseph adopted Jesus into the line of Adam. That is how a second opportunity to win the battle came to pass.

Jesus lived a perfect life and never sinned, even once. When he died on the cross, he took the punishment for the sins of all God's children. To prove his victory over death, Jesus rose from the dead. Jesus became the representative head for all who believe and put their trust in him. God forgives those who trust in his Son Jesus and adopts them into his family as brothers and sisters of Christ.

Pride tells us that we can work our way to heaven by our good works (or that God's judgment is just a made-up story). But God in the Bible teaches us that standing before him and having to give an account of our lives is not a made-up story. The moment you sin once, you've spoiled your perfect record and become a sinner. The only way to get to heaven is to have your sin removed. The only way to remove your sin is to trust what Jesus did upon the cross, in your place, as your representative. Through his victory over sin, anyone who turns from his or her sin to Jesus can be forgiven.

But Jesus is the last person the dragon of old wants you to trust. He has a cunning way of fooling people. Satan wants to fool you into thinking you don't need to trust in Jesus, that you are good enough on your own, and if you try hard enough God will let you into heaven. If that lie doesn't work, he has another one for you—that Jesus wasn't God and we won't have to stand before God one day to give an account of our lives. But those are lies from the pit of hell. The truth is that we will all have to answer to our Creator and our good works can't erase our sins. That is why we need to trust in Jesus who lived a perfect life as our representative. Will you trust him?

WHAT ABOUT YOU?

1. Think through the past week or so. Where have you failed to obey God's Word? (think about the ten commandments for a start) Have you lied, disobeyed or disrespected those in authority over you? Have you gotten angry because you didn't get what you wanted?

2. Once a person realizes they are a sinner and need God to forgive them, what can they do? (If you are not sure look up this Bible verse: Acts 17:29–31.)

3. Read through Ephesians 2:1–9. What does it say about how we are saved from our sin?

Day Five

The Prophecy Is True

For to us a child is born, to us a son is given; and the government shall be upon his shoulder, and his name shall be called Wonderful Counselor, Mighty God, Everlasting Father, Prince of Peace.

Isaiah 9:6

A Bedouin shepherd, searching for a lost goat, spotted a cave, cut into the mountains west of the Dead Sea in Israel. Allowing his curiosity to overcome caution, the shepherd climbed the jagged rock. Once in the mouth of the cave, it is said that he stumbled and landed on a clay jar, full of seven scrolls.

Unaware of the importance of the sheepskin parchments, he took the scrolls home and placed his discovery on display in his tent. One of the scrolls contained a near-complete manuscript of the writings of the prophet Isaiah. Believing his discovery would make him some money, he tried to sell the scrolls, but was told that the tattered scrolls he found were worthless. In the end, the shepherd sold the scrolls for a few dollars. They changed hands several times until a researcher recognized their true value.

Up until that point, the oldest copy of Isaiah was dated hundreds of years after the death of Christ. The book of Isaiah contained verse after verse of detailed prophecy, predicting the coming of a sin-bearer. These prophecies described Jesus perfectly. He would be born of a virgin, both man and God, who would die to take the punishment we deserved for our sins. Many people thought that these prophecies were too accurate to have been written before Jesus's birth.

But the Isaiah's scroll that was discovered in that cave was more than a thousand years older than the oldest copy and dated at least 150 years before the birth of Christ, proving beyond doubt, the prophecy was true.

Frayed along the edges, two lines up from a tear, the words of today's Bible verse are clear and readable.

> For to us a child is born, to us a son is given; and the government shall be upon his shoulder, and his name shall be called Wonderful Counselor, Mighty God, Everlasting Father, Prince of Peace.

There can be no doubt that Isaiah prophesied the coming of Christ hundreds of years before his birth. His prophecy predicted that a child born to man would also be "Mighty God." Do you see that in the verse? A "child" is born; a baby boy carried in the womb of his mom until birth. But this child, born a man, would also be "Mighty God." There, in this one verse, God revealed to Isaiah his plan. And Isaiah lived and wrote these words more than 600 years before Jesus was born.

So why do people still doubt and not believe? One word describes the reason: pride. People do not want to humble themselves and follow God, so they refuse to believe. The devil, who hates God, is ever ready to whisper his approval into their ear. One of the Dragon's greatest lies is to tell you that the Bible is not true because it was written by men. But God tells us that while men did write the Scriptures, they were inspired by the Holy Spirit and calls the words of the Bible "God Breathed," (2 Timothy 3:16).

WHAT ABOUT YOU?

1. Read chapters 7 and 53 in the book of Isaiah. Make a list of what Isaiah predicted about Jesus 600 years before he was born.

2. How could Isaiah know about Jesus 600 years before he was born? How does knowing Isaiah's prophecy affect the way you think about the Bible?

3. Look up 2 Timothy 3:16 and 2 Peter 1:21. How do these verses describe the way God used men to write his words?

Day Six

Humility: The Antidote to Pride

Do nothing from selfish ambition or conceit, but in humility count others more significant than yourselves. Let each of you look not only to his own interests, but also to the interests of others. Have this mind among yourselves, which is yours in Christ Jesus, who, though he was in the form of God, did not count equality with God a thing to be grasped, but emptied himself, by taking the form of a servant, being born in the likeness of men. And being found in human form, he humbled himself by becoming obedient to the point of death, even death on a cross.

Philippians 2:3–8

Children love to boast. Kids challenge one another to prove who is taller or arm wrestle to show who is stronger. Pride is always at work in our heart tempting us to show off our own greatness.

But one teenage boy, Edouard Beaupré, didn't have to challenge anyone concerning height or strength. For as soon as he entered a room everyone could see he was the tallest and strongest. Edouard stood over eight feet tall. By the age of seventeen, he could lift an 800-pound horse with his bare hands. Edouard joined the circus to show off his great prowess as a strong man.

But as strong as Edouard was, he was not the strongest man to ever live; Jesus was. As the Son of God, Jesus had command over the universe. Consider these biblical descriptions of him.

> He is the radiance of the glory of God and the exact imprint of his nature, and he upholds the universe by the word of his power. (Hebrews 1:3)

> For by him all things were created . . . and in him all things hold together. (Colossians 1:16–17)

In spite of his eternal greatness, Jesus didn't boast. Philippians 2 describes how the Son of God humbled himself by giving up his glory to become a man and then live in humility serving others all his days.

Think about that. Jesus had more to boast and show off about than any person who ever lived. But he resisted the temptations to boast. He never used his strength against others or to make himself great—not even against those who nailed him to the cross. Jesus came to win the war against sin with the greatest display of humility for all time.

So what about us? Will we believe in Jesus and boast about him? Or will we lift our own name and interests higher and boast of our greatness? That is the challenge the passage from Philippians 2 gives us. But we can't break the power of pride in our lives on our own. We need Jesus's help.

You see, Jesus took our sin when he humbled himself all the way to death. He died to break the power of boasting in the life of anyone who will trust in him. Jesus won the battle against sinful pride and now, as you ask him for help, he gives us the power to follow him. It takes humility to admit you are a sinner and ask Jesus to forgive you. Pride is always eager to try to convince us that we can handle things on our own. But don't listen to the voice of pride; listen to the Word of God. Follow in Jesus's steps. Ask for the Spirit to remind you even when you are in the middle of boasting that you can walk like Jesus did. Practice humility for it is humility that restrains our pride.

Since humility is the opposite of pride, it is the last thing the Dragon wants you to have. When you humble yourself and follow God, it neutralizes his temptations. For example, the enemy wants you to hide your sin and keep it in the darkness, but humility directs you to confess your sin and bring it out into the light. The enemy knows he can tempt you into more sin (like lying about what you did) if you keep your sin hidden. But once you follow the path of humility and bring your sin into the light, the enemy's temptation to lie about your sin has no power over you.

WHAT ABOUT YOU?

1. When (or where) are you most tempted to boast? Think about the situations you are in when you want to boast. What do you hope to get? Or to avoid?

2. Paul tells us to consider the interests of others instead of just thinking about ourselves. What does it look like in your life to consider the interests of others? Who would that be, your brother or sister, your parents, your friends?

3. Can you remember a time when you wrestled with whether or not you should confess a secret sin? How did it feel to hide it? How did it feel to humble yourself and confess it?

Day Seven

God Knows Your Struggle

Since then we have a great high priest who has passed through the heavens, Jesus, the Son of God, let us hold fast our confession. For we do not have a high priest who is unable to sympathize with our weaknesses, but one who in every respect has been tempted as we are, yet without sin. Let us then with confidence draw near to the throne of grace, that we may receive mercy and find grace to help in time of need.

Hebrews 4:14–16

The saying, "Don't judge a man until you have walked a mile in his shoes" is said to have originated with the Native Americans. The meaning of this saying is simple. We shouldn't be quick to judge or criticize other people because we may not understand how difficult their life is.

The greatest sympathy and understanding comes from walking in their shoes, which means sharing the same struggle. It is easy to judge a person for getting a *D* in Physics when you've never taken the class yourself. Once you understand how difficult the class is, you are less likely to criticize others. It is a whole lot easier to understand how hard it is to recover from having your wisdom teeth extracted once you've lived through it yourself. Why? Because we "walked a mile" in their shoes.

Hebrews 4 reminds us that Jesus walked a mile in our shoes. Jesus does know how hard it is to fight the temptations of sin and pride because he had to fight those same temptations. God knows the power of pride to destroy us and gives us grace to battle when we call upon him in prayer.

Jesus is not critical of us as we battle with temptations because he knows how hard it is. Instead of being critical, Jesus invites us to run to him with our struggles. This is what he says to us in the Bible:

> Come to me, all who labor and are heavy laden, and I will give you rest. Take my yoke upon you, and learn from me, for I am gentle and lowly in heart, and you will find rest for your souls. For my yoke is easy, and my burden is light. (Matthew 11:28–30)

The Dragon tries to condemn us in our sin. He is called the accuser of the brethren (Revelation 12:10). He wants us to believe we are not worthy to call out to Jesus—that our sins are too great to ever be forgiven. But the writer of Hebrews tells us the truth—that Jesus walked the same path we walk. He understands how difficult life is and how hard it is to say no to the world's sinful pleasures and the enemy's temptations. So we can run to Jesus with our struggles, knowing he welcomes us and will help us.

WHAT ABOUT YOU?

1. Have you ever prayed to God about your struggles and asked him to help you? Where do you need his help today?

2. Why do you think it is so hard to start your day asking Jesus for help? (Consider the role your pride and Satan's temptations might have in this.)

3. Brainstorm some ways that will help you remember to start out each day asking Jesus to help you.

Day Eight

No One Is Invincible

Brothers and sisters, if someone is caught in a sin, you who live by the Spirit should restore that person gently. But watch yourselves, or you also may be tempted. Carry each other's burdens, and in this way you will fulfill the law of Christ. If anyone thinks they are something when they are not, they deceive themselves.

Galatians 6:1–3 NIV

Promotional advertisements for the Titanic said the ship was "designed to be unsinkable." Today the Titanic rests at the bottom of the ocean.

It sank on its maiden voyage after striking an iceberg. Engineers designed other ships with a double hull. That way if something cut through the first layer of steel, a second layer kept the vessel floating. Fifty years earlier, the Great Eastern suffered a similar accident when a rock ripped an eighty-foot long, nine-foot wide gash in its side. But the double wall construction of the Great Eastern kept the damaged vessel afloat with no loss of life. To maximize space, engineers of the Titanic did not include the double wall design that would have kept it from sinking. They never thought their ship would crash into an iceberg.

Their attitude reminds me a little bit of the story Jesus told about the prayers of the Tax Collector and the Pharisee. Do you remember how the Pharisee's prayer showed how he thought he was so much better than the Tax Collector? The Pharisee said, "I thank you that I am not like other men, extortioners, unjust, adulterers, or even like this tax collector. I fast twice a week; I give tithes of all that I get" (Luke 18:11–12). His boasting sounds a bit like the advertisement for the Titanic. It was as though the Pharisee were saying, "I'm so glad that I am unsinkable."

We shouldn't compare our lives to others who are struggling and think we are doing pretty well. Instead, we should only compare ourselves to God, who is perfectly holy and without sin. When we compare ourselves to others, we can be fooled into thinking we don't need to watch out for sin. But when we compare ourselves to God, we realize we are sinners, who need God's help.

The builders of the Titanic thought they didn't need a double hull. One person on board is reported to have said, "Even God couldn't sink this ship." But the judgment of the iceberg came. On that fateful day, the passengers discovered how they had been deceived, for the Titanic didn't have enough lifeboats for all to escape. As a result, many more people died. They thought they were safe—that their ship would never fail—then the iceberg came.

Let's not make that same mistake. You are only safe in Christ.

WHAT ABOUT YOU?

1. What is the danger of looking at another person's struggle and saying to yourself, "I would never do that?"

2. Why do we like to compare ourselves with those around?

3. Look up Romans 12:3. Where in your life are you most likely to think you don't need help when perhaps you really do?

Day Nine

True Greatness

When he had washed their feet and put on his outer garments and resumed his place, he said to them, "Do you understand what I have done to you? You call me Teacher and Lord, and you are right, for so I am. If I then, your Lord and Teacher, have washed your feet, you also ought to wash one another's feet. For I have given you an example, that you also should do just as I have done to you. Truly, truly, I say to you, a servant is not greater than his master, nor is a messenger greater than the one who sent him. If you know these things, blessed are you if you do them."

John 13:12–17

At age twelve, Apa Sherpa's father died, forcing him to leave school to find work to provide for his family. Apa, who lived high in the mountains of Nepal, took a job as a mountain porter, carrying equipment and supplies for climbers. Apa carried heavy loads up the slope of Mount Everest for twelve years before ever taking the last leg of the climb to the summit.

Mountain climbers, celebrating their victory atop the world's highest peak, had Apa to thank for their success. God rewarded Apa for his humility. For the longer he worked, the stronger and more experienced he became. In time, Apa did make it to the summit. Today, with twenty-one climbs of Everest, Apa holds the world record. While most people climb Mount Everest for their own glory, Apa has given his life to serving, using many of his later expeditions to pick up the trash left behind by other mountain climbers. His efforts and those of others he has inspired have removed over thirty thousand pounds of trash from the mountain.

The disciples often argued which of one of them was the greatest. Luke tells us that the disciples argued the night before Jesus's death on the cross. To teach them humility, Jesus took up a towel and a basin and washed their dirty feet. Washing feet was a task for the lowest of servants, a job no one wanted to do.

Jesus wanted to teach them that humility is the path to true greatness. The foot-washing he performed was nothing compared to the suffering upon the cross he faced later. It was on the cross, the greatest demonstration of humility of all time, where Jesus carried our sins upon his back. God the Father punished Jesus in our place. Jesus died to take the blame for the sins of all those who repent of pride and place their trust in his saving work.

You can't climb Everest alone; you need to humble yourself and hire a guide and porters to carry your equipment. You can't get to heaven alone; you need to humble yourself, and trust in Jesus who died for you. What will win out in your life, the pride of sinful independence or humility? The choice is yours.

Once again, let me warn you that the Dragon will do all he can to convince you that you are good enough—that you do not need "religion." He will want you to believe that you can believe in God but don't have to trust in Jesus. Be very careful, for James tells us that the demons believe in God—they know there is a God, but they are not going to heaven because they don't love or trust God and they hate Jesus (James 2:19).

WHAT ABOUT YOU?

1. How do you answer that last question? What will win out in your life, the pride of sinful independence or humility?

2. Who has most helped you in life? Have you ever thanked them for their help to acknowledge that you could would not have made it if it were not for them?

3. What is the difference in saying you believe in God and trusting Jesus for your salvation?

Day Ten

His Story Is History

Now from the sixth hour there was darkness over all the land until the ninth hour. And about the ninth hour Jesus cried out with a loud voice, saying, "Eli, Eli, lema sabachthani?" that is, "My God, my God, why have you forsaken me?" And some of the bystanders, hearing it, said, "This man is calling Elijah." And one of them at once ran and took a sponge, filled it with sour wine, and put it on a reed and gave it to him to drink. But the others said, "Wait, let us see whether Elijah will come to save him." And Jesus cried out again with a loud voice and yielded up his spirit.
And behold, the curtain of the temple was torn in two, from top to bottom. And the earth shook, and the rocks were split. The tombs also were opened. And many bodies of the saints who had fallen asleep were raised, and coming out of the tombs after his resurrection they went into the holy city and appeared to many. When the centurion and those who were with him, keeping watch over Jesus, saw the earthquake and what took place, they were filled with awe and said, "Truly this was the Son of God!"

Matthew 27:45–54

The John Rylands' fragment is the oldest known portion of the New Testament ever found. Scientists estimate it was written only thirty-five years after John first penned his Gospel. While all other ancient history books have less than a dozen surviving fragments or copies, there are over 5,500 copies and fragments of the New Testament with many of them written less than 100 years from the time the original was completed. That is why the manuscripts so closely agree and are nearly perfect copies of one another.

So when we read the historical account from Matthew's Gospel of what happened after the crucifixion, we can trust it is true. The four Gospels were not written hundreds of years after these events. They were written a few years after the events they describe. In fact, Matthew and John were firsthand witnesses of all that took place. So you see, the account of Jesus's death and resurrection is not fiction or fable; the story of Jesus is history, as true as ruins of ancient Rome tell us of the once-great nation.

So when they tell us, as in Matthew 27, that they saw Jesus die on the cross, we can trust that it happened. When they tell us that the earth grew dark and shook at his death, and the temple curtain tore from top to bottom, we can trust it is true. The temple curtain blocked the way into the presence of God in the Holy of Holies. When God ripped the curtain, he was telling us that he opened the way to forgiveness. Jesus's death on the cross paid for the sins of his people and opened the way for all of us who believe to live with God and enjoy his presence without the fear of judgment.

With only seven surviving copies of his writing, no one doubts the authenticity of Plato's writing. Nor do they doubt Aristotle's writings, though the earliest copy found is 1200 years older than the original. But millions of people refuse to believe the authenticity of the New Testament. Why? Why do so many people refuse to believe? Why do people say the Scriptures are unreliable and untrustworthy? By now you should know there is a one-word answer: pride. They choose to believe what they want to believe, instead of what God's Word says. Anytime our thinking goes against what the Word of God teaches, we can be certain that pride has gotten a hold on us.

WHAT ABOUT YOU?

1. When we agree that the Bible is an accurate historical record, it forces us to accept the eye-witness testimony of men who said Jesus rose from the dead and they saw him. Why is the resurrection so important?

2. If someone were asked to observe your life for one week, would they say you believe that the Bible is God's Word?

3. Read Hebrews 4:12. What makes the Bible different than other history books?

Day Eleven

What No Other Man Has Done

Now after the Sabbath, toward the dawn of the first day of the week, Mary Magdalene and the other Mary went to see the tomb. And behold, there was a great earthquake, for an angel of the Lord descended from heaven and came and rolled back the stone and sat on it. His appearance was like lightning, and his clothing white as snow. And for fear of him the guards trembled and became like dead men. But the angel said to the women, "Do not be afraid, for I know that you seek Jesus who was crucified. He is not here, for he has risen, as he said. Come, see the place where he lay. Then go quickly and tell his disciples that he has risen from the dead, and behold, he is going before you to Galilee; there you will see him. See, I have told you."

Matthew 28:1–7

There is one fact about Jesus that makes him different from every other religious ruler, prophet, or holy man. Jesus rose from the dead. If you were to dig up the grave of any other religious leader, you would find the remains of his body buried there. But

Jesus's tomb is empty and the resurrection of Jesus Christ from the dead is the greatest miracle in history.

Matthew 28 describes the resurrection of Jesus Christ from the dead. Imagine being the first to the tomb only to find it empty! Imagine hearing the angel announce that Jesus rose from the dead, just as he said he would. Even though we are living almost 2000 years after the resurrection, we should be just as amazed.

Think of it. The resurrection stands as the single greatest proof that Jesus's claims about himself are true. Jesus was not just a man. He claimed to be the Son of God and is one with the Father (John 10:30). Jesus said he was the only way to the Father in heaven (John 14:6).

Not only that but Jesus predicted his death. He told his disciples that "he must go to Jerusalem and suffer many things from the elders and chief priests and scribes, and be killed, and on the third day be raised" (Matthew 16:21). Jesus even knew he would be crucified. He told his disciples if they wanted to follow him, they would need to pick up their cross (Matthew 16:24). Jesus said that he laid his life down freely and could take it back up again (John 10:18).

Right after the resurrection the enemy was up to his tricks again. The religious leaders met with the soldiers who stood guard at the tomb. They gave them money to lie and tell everyone that the disciples came in the night and stole Jesus's body (Matthew 28:12–13).

Today we are all called to believe in Jesus. It is only our pride that would lead us to trust ourselves and reject Jesus.

WHAT ABOUT YOU?

1. Why do people reject the Bible's account of the resurrection of Jesus?

2. What do you believe about Jesus and the resurrection?

3. Read 1 Corinthians 15:12–19. Why does Paul say that the physical resurrection of Jesus from the dead is so vital to our faith?

Day Twelve

Humility Kills the Dragon

Humble yourselves, therefore, under the mighty hand of God so that at the proper time he may exalt you, casting all your anxieties on him, because he cares for you. Be sober-minded; be watchful. Your adversary the devil prowls around like a roaring lion, seeking someone to devour. Resist him, firm in your faith, knowing that the same kinds of suffering are being experienced by your brotherhood throughout the world. And after you have suffered a little while, the God of all grace, who has called you to his eternal glory in Christ, will himself restore, confirm, strengthen, and establish you. To him be the dominion forever and ever. Amen.

1 Peter 5:6–11

The famous baseball player Babe Ruth was Billy Frank's hero. By the time Billy reached the age of sixteen, Babe Ruth had hit over 700 home runs, more than any other man in history. Babe Ruth was also one of the greatest left-handed pitchers of all time. Few baseball players could claim fame both in hitting and in pitching. Perhaps that is why Billy looked up to Ruth.

But Billy's hero changed abruptly during a revival meeting he attended with a friend when he was sixteen. He had heard there might be a disturbance at the meeting and came to watch out of curiosity. He sat behind the preacher so the evangelist couldn't point his finger at him. But even though he sat behind the preacher, Billy felt the evangelist's words speaking to him and came back a second night to hear more. It was at that second meeting that Billy humbled himself and gave his life to serving his new hero, Jesus Christ. Most people know Billy Frank by his full name, William Franklin Graham. Better known as Billy Graham.

Our Bible verse today is very similar to the one from our first study: "God opposes the proud but gives grace to the humble" (James 4:6). In today's verse, Peter tells us to humble ourselves, and he adds a sober warning. The devil is at work, prowling around, looking for people to destroy. Humility is our weapon against his evil schemes. If we humble ourselves, Peter promises, God will exalt us. That doesn't mean our lives will be easy. We will still have trials. But in the end, at the final judgment, we will not suffer punishment.

Billy Graham chose humility over pride and became a preacher. Billy Graham has preached the gospel of Jesus Christ to hundreds of millions of proud young men and women and millions have responded by humbling themselves, turning away from their sin, and following Christ.

The antidote to the horrible affects of sinful pride is humility—confessing our sin and need for Jesus to save us. Each one of us has a choice to make. Will we trust in Jesus to take our sin away or reject Jesus and live for ourselves? The dragon will do all he can to tempt you away from trusting in Jesus. He will tell you that you have plenty of time, that you don't have to be so radical, that not everyone trusts in Jesus, that God isn't real, the Bible is written by men, and a thousand other lies and temptations. But there is one thing about these lies—they never change. They are always the same. The apostle Paul wrote: "No temptation has overtaken you that is not common to man. God is faithful, and he will not let you be tempted beyond your ability, but with the temptation he will also provide the way of escape, that you may be able to endure it." (1 Corinthians 10:13)

So, when you hear these familiar temptations from others or think them yourself, reject them and run to God. Humble yourself, confess your sin and trust in Jesus. When you resist the temptations of the enemy he will flee (James 4:7) and you will be saved.

WHAT ABOUT YOU?

1. What about you? What will you do with your life? Will you fight the dragon with humility by giving your life to Christ, or will you give into pride and allow its seeds to grow and twist their evil roots down deep within your heart?

2. What has affected you the most in this book? What is one thing you can do to draw closer to God?

3. Find other people who have conquered the Dragon by trusting in Jesus and ask them to share their story with you.